Resurrection 2027

by J.G. Eccarius

III Publishing
P.O. Box 1581
Gualala, CA 95445

1st Printing: May 1995

Cover Design by Bill Meyers

The publisher and author wish to extend special thanks to Jan Edwards and Elizabeth Ann Lockhart for proofreading, and to Zack, Mike, Bill and George for feedback.

ISBN 0-9622937-7-6

Our motto: the only good lawyer is a dead lawyer.

This is not an ordinary book. It is written in ordinary language, because that is a language you understand. But it is an organism, suspended in time, in black ink on white paper (or bits of light or electricity if you downloaded this), an organism waiting for a host. You are the host.

The human body is nothing but a host. A host for you, for languages, for knowledge, for feelings, for ecstasy and terror, boredom and relief.

This book is an illusion, but it opens the gate to reality.

The organism you are about to imbibe is woven so cleverly into the book, and will weave so cleverly into your mind, that you will think you always had it. Its blood is the heat of human passion, its flesh is a thousand cities, and its nerves are words and echoes of words.

Enjoy.

Chapter 1

"Blessed be Mary the Mother of God! Children, wake up!"

The bell clanged in Mother Elizabeth's hand and Ann, already awake, tossed off her bedsheet. By the time the bell stopped her feet aimed her down the path between the row of beds. Despite her bed's distant location she moved quickly enough to not have to stand in line in the washroom. A few robed bodies had managed to get ahead of her, but most of the girls waited behind her. A few had to be slapped by Mother before they came to, the same as every morning.

A long shelf with a dozen holes in it served as a toilet. Across from it stood an equally long metal trench with a dozen faucets and tiny mirrors of varied shapes mounted above it. There were also showers, but the girls were not allowed to use them in the morning. Ann took one of the toilets, then waited behind Mary Johnson in order to use a sink. The water touched her with shocking cold when she washed her face. In the mirror her hair reflected light brown, her eyes blue, her skin a mushroom's paleness. She liked her face, it was long and had a fine nose.

She walked back, made her bed, and changed into her school uniform: blue pants held up by a tie-string and a long sleeved white shirt with buttons going down the front. Since she was skinny the clothing hung very loosely on her. She wished she could go straight to eat, or at least get in the front of a line to leave, but the rule was that all the girls had to stand by the beds until they had passed the first of Mother Elizabeth's daily inspections. This involved seeing that the beds were made properly and that the girls were clean and properly dressed.

In the cafeteria line she received her bowl of hot cereal. Tomorrow, she reminded herself, was a sugar day, and there would be sugar with breakfast. She thrilled to think of it. She was so lucky; before the Apocalypse and the Resurrection people had not had sugar but perhaps twice a year.

The first class of the day was history. This year, for the first time, they read history as a topic separate from Remembrance or Theology. Mother Katherine Ann taught it in overview, from the beginning of time when God created the earth up to the present. Halfway into the school year they studied the Middle Ages. The first half of class consisted of reading the textbook; the second would be listening to Mother Katherine Ann, answering questions, and writing a short essay. Ann quickly skimmed over the section they were supposed to read; she had read it carefully weeks earlier. Then she went on to read ahead in the book. That was against the rules, but she did it anyway.

She was excited because she was almost to the second half of the 20th century. Soon she would read up to the year of her birth, 1970, and read about the world she had lived in so long ago. Of course she already remembered quite a bit about her life before Resurrection; that was what Remembrance classes were for. She had been raised from the dead in 2013; she was 14 years resurrected.

The ancient struggle between Good and Evil, God and the Devil, Mother Mary and the Anti-Christs had come to a head during Ann's prior lifetime. In the preceding decades the atomic bomb had been invented and the ecocrisis gathered in intensity. Even in God's chosen nation, the United States of America, the contest was severe. Christians divided into many sects, most led by bad men. Anti-Christs were everywhere, including in the Government. Few people were prepared for the Apocalypse and the Second Coming. People watched Anti-Christ preachers on Television rather than obeying Mary the Mother of Christ and her priestesses. Technology was advanced by men guided by Satan and bent on destroying the world. There were many wars: Korea, Vietnam, the wars in the Middle East and Africa. Communist-atheists, agents of the devil, took over the island of Cuba. The government of the United States persecuted, imprisoned and tortured Christians. The Bible could not be taught in schools, and Christians had to pay taxes to support the government's anti-Christian propaganda campaigns. Still, many people were true to the faith, or tried to be true despite their confusion.

Before Ann reached the years between her birth and the Apocalypse the time for reading was over.

But her teacher pulled her outside of the classroom at the end of the lesson."Ann, Mother Mary Rebecca wishes to speak to you. Please go straight to her office," said Mother Katherine Ann.

"Yes, Mother." Ann was instantly terror-struck. I must have done something wrong, she thought. Had Mother Katherine Ann seen her reading ahead in the history book? Had God told them her secret thoughts, the ones that she tried not to think?

It was not a long walk to Mother Mary Rebecca's office, but Ann examined almost every thought she had during the preceding few days.

Mother Mary Rebecca was a tall woman; taller than Ann and most of the teenage Children in Ann's class, even taller than the other Mothers. To Ann she seemed very old. Ann was sure that when Christ and Mother Mary came to earth to end the Apocalypse Mother Mary Rebecca had been one of the witnesses. As head Mother of the Holy Redeemer School and Womb of Mary VII Child Care Facility, Mary Rebecca functioned as its ultimate disciplinarian.

The Head Mother's body sat enshrouded in the same clothing all the Mothers wore: a loose black robe that reached from the neck to the ground. Except for her height she was recognizable only by her face, a long oval set with a small nose, eyes and lips. Her eyes flashed pale blue; piercing as only those whose authority is unquestioned can be.

"Ann, angel, come in."

"Yes, Mother Mary Rebecca."

Mother Mary Rebecca gazed at her a while, saying nothing.

"You have done very well in your classes, Ann. God has blessed you."

"Yes, Mother Mary Rebecca."

"Before the Apocalypse you were a nurse." Mother waited.

"Yes, Mother Mary Rebecca."

"Do you know what a nurse is?"

"Yes, Mother Mary Rebecca. A nurse is a woman who takes care of the sick, following a doctor's orders."

"That is correct, Ann. But there are many things about nursing and medicine that you have not recalled yet. To be a good nurse or doctor requires the study of the human body. You have already made those studies in your past life, so it should be easy for you to recall them. However, you are not to become a nurse, at least not now. God has ordered that the pace of Resurrection be increased. Resurrection is one of Mother Mary's miracles, but we act as her servants in this process. For more resurrections, there must be more servants. You have been chosen for this special service. Tomorrow morning you will be sent to a special school in Resurrection City for this great purpose. Now it would be best if you go to the chapel and pray for guidance until lights out."

Again Mother Mary Rebecca paused.

"Yes, Mother Mary Rebecca."

"Why did God resurrect you, Ann?"

"To know her and to love her."

"That is correct. One way you will learn to know her and love her is through doing her work. You may go."

The Chapel was large enough for all 400 students at Holy Redeemer to sit in at once. Ann knelt there alone. She had never been there alone before.

She thanked God for resurrecting her. Then she went through some standard, memorized prayers: Thanks to Jesus, Mother Mary's Prayer, Cast Out Wickedness, and others they had learned at the school. But then she started wondering about her history book: why had things been so bad before the Apocalypse? And why had she been killed, martyred, only to be resurrected 15 years later? What would it be like in the special school? Maybe her questions would be answered.

She already had new questions. Why was not she resurrected as an adult, since she had died as an adult? Why did only teachers ask questions, why not the students? Why did God resurrect people a few at a time, rather than all at once, and why more now than before?

She had no basis to answer these questions, no knowledge of anything outside of Holy Redeemer and before that the Womb of Mary VII infant care facility, nothing beyond the companionship of her sister Children, the books they read, and the authority of the Mothers. She felt, was sure, something major was missing from this life, but believed that God, through the Mothers, would supply it at some point, just as they had supplied her with all of her needs. After all, they had rescued her from death itself.

The next morning her day started as usual, but was quickly interrupted. Mother Elizabeth asked her to wait in the bunk room when the other girls went off to breakfast. A short time passed and Mother Elizabeth returned with a woman dressed as a Saint. She wore a yellowed, long-sleeved shirt and a long yellow skirt that hung loosely about her legs. She was not one of the Saints who worked for the Mothers at Holy Redeemer.

"This is Ann Swanson. Ann, this is Saint Mary Jones, who will take you to the Temple of Resurrection. We are all proud to see you go, and expect you will be a glory to Mary the Mother of God."

"Yes Mother Elizabeth."

"Pick up your things." And while Ann went for her tiny bag of belongings Mother Elizabeth left.

"This way, dearie," said Saint Mary Jones.

Ann wanted to ask why Mary dressed as she did, but she had never asked anyone a question aloud in her life, so she just followed the woman. They went through a door that led to the kitchen, but bypassed the kitchen and went though another door down a long hall. Mary started rising into the air. It took a moment for Ann to realize that Mary was walking on ... something ... Ann raised her foot, focused her eyes on the step, set her foot down, moved her body up a step, saw Mary receding, and took a second step up, unsteady. Mary looked back, smiling.

"Have you been up these steps before, dear?" Mary said.

"No. Is this a staircase?" Ann asked the question without thinking, and to her surprise Mary did not seem to notice.

"That is right, dear. You will be seeing stranger things. Move along now, I will be in trouble if we are late."

Ann negotiated the steps up to Mary only to have Mary start off again in the opposite direction, around a turn. There were several flights of steps and Ann's legs hurt long before they reached the top.

They emérged through another door into a room almost as big as the chapel. A large metal machine dominated the room; after a moment, following Saint Mary Jones, Ann realized there were two separate machines. Mary opened one up.

"You have to get inside, in the seat," she said.

Ann looked into the machine, saw a seat, and managed to get into it. Mary closed the door and Ann saw small windows she could see out of. Before she could get her bearings Mary opened the machine from the other side and got in.

"It is old," Mary said, "but it runs. Do not worry, it is not a long trip."

Chapter 2

Mary Kate Ashton watched the graph on the screen reach upward and turn red, indicating another failed run. She swayed suddenly as a clapping sound filled the air. It took her a fraction of a second – a subjectively long fraction of a second – to realize that the building itself was swaying. All of the muscles of her body tensed and she felt as if she was shrinking inward as another fraction of time passed, then another. The swaying stopped.

As her eyes started to scan the room she noticed her hands braced against the computer keyboard. Pulling back her hands and starting to stand up she ignored the changed screen of the computer. Mary Kate walked from one end of the room to the other, looking at things, picking up an occasional tool or pencil from the floor. Focusing her mind so, she ignored the novel bodily sensations of anxiety floating inside her and beneath her skin. She looked at everything, the tables, cabinets, computers, even the doors and lights. All seemed normal.

She could not think of what the shaking room could have been. It meant something and it had to be something, but what? Probably the Mothers would know. Perhaps it was a sort of test. If she went to Mother Sarah Ruth she might be sent right back. After all, she was supposed to finish her work. God's work.

A few minutes had passed when she sat back down to work. Before her a strange screen read "Welcome to the Magic Librarian Encyclopedia Database. If you need help, press F1." The menu was short: the choices were Version and Subject, which meant nothing to her. In fact she recognized only 'Librarian' and 'Database'; 'Magic' and 'Encyclopedia' were new words to her. She could quit the program by pressing the F10 or Escape key.

Her first thought was that she was somewhere in the system she was not supposed to be. But then, what had the shaking been about? Surely nothing could shake the room but God. Maybe it had not been the room She shook but the city or even all of heaven, the whole planet earth. Or maybe God just wanted Mary Kate to see the Magic Librarian.

She decided she needed help.

The help menu did not clear up what an encyclopedia was, but it listed eight of them: *Britannica, Groliers, Americana,* etc. Most of the choices had numbers after them that appeared to be old style, pre-Apocalypse year numbers. The latest was the year before the Apocalypse, 2000 old style. The earliest was the first *Britannica*, numbered 1910.

There was also a dictionary. She knew what a dictionary was. The help menu said you choose a version of Encyclopedia and then can choose a subject, or you can choose a subject and see what the various versions said about it. She decided to start by choosing the dictionary and asking it for the subject "encyclopedia."

Deciphering that an encyclopedia is like a dictionary except each subject has an article about it instead of just a definition, she back tracked to the main menu and chose the Encyclopedia Americana because she knew Zion was called the United States of America before the Apocalypse. Mary Kate selected the most recent version, 1997, and then asked for Encyclopedia when prompted for a subject.

Reading, she gathered that there had been many encyclopedia's written over a long period of time. Since she knew little of history (though she thought she knew all there was to know) and no philosophy, it was the first time she heard of Plato, Cato, and other figures. She did not understand the word "controversy" or why so much was written about the *Encyclopedie* edited by Diderot that appeared in 1751. Several of the encyclopedias in the Magic Library were mentioned, including the Britannica.

Somehow the subject "encyclopedia" was not what God intended her to look at, she concluded. But what subject was?

It also occurred to her that bedtime was close and she still had much work to do. She tried to balance that against the possibility that she would never find the Magic Library again. Perhaps if she explained it all to Mother. But if God wanted Mother to help her, then why did she use such a strange method? Perhaps it was only an accident. Perhaps it was not God who shook the room. Or God shook the room, but not to show her the library.

She decided to try one more subject. Cleveland. Where she was born and lived before the Apocalypse. There were several choices for Cleveland, which was odd and confusing for a moment, but she picked the city.

The Encyclopedia said that Cleveland had a population of a half million people. That was impossible. She had never asked what the population had been before the Apocalypse, and she did not remember from her past life, but she doubted there were a hundred thousand people in all of Zion. And they lived in many cities. Surely, many people had died in the Apocalypse, but certainly so many people could not have lived upon the earth. Why, virtually everyone must have been followers of the Anti-Christ. Perhaps.

The rest of the entry was equally confusing. It made so little sense to her she might as well have been reading French: it seemed like it should make sense.

She decided to leave the Magic Library. When she hit the F10 key to "quit" the library, however, she did not end up in the familiar System. Instead a screen read: If you wish to change your password, enter your new password here. To keep your old password, hit Enter.

Password Mary Kate understood. She changed it to MAGIC. That would be easy to remember.

She was back in the System. Before she asked for her regular menu she typed in MAGIC. She was taken to the library. Simple enough. People probably used the encyclopedias all the time. There just was no need in her case.

Mary Kate prepared to make another run at the troubling gene sequence, the one that had failed just before the room shook.

Chapter 3

Jake Thompson put his right knee forward for the thousandth time that day. A great leather patch on his pants, and skin almost as tough over his kneecap, sank slightly into the loamy soil. Jake grabbed a weed, a baby thistle plant, digging his fingers down to tear it out by the root. He tossed the plant into a sack; it would not go to waste. The corn flanking him and extending in long rows before and behind him stood no higher than his waist. Overhead was a canopy of thin, clear plastic, supported by occasional plastic pillars and cross-beams.

When he came to an older thistle, one with a head about to bloom, he bit the head off as the plant passed from soil to his sack. It tasted bitter as he chewed; most weeds did. He figured the head had some nutritional value, like an artichoke. Perhaps one could live entirely on weeds; could it be any worse than the bread and corn-gruel diet to which he had grown so accustomed?

Jake had noticed that outside the crop houses there were weeds coming back. At first, years before, he had not been sure because it was a slow process and there had always been some weeds. But now he was sure.

Jake was a slider, he always had been. It would have been impossible to tell by watching him now, at the age of 48. He worked steady for two hours, then took the brief allotted break, then repeated the routine four times. But that was as close to sliding as he could get in Zion. Jake Thompson valued his life. He had never slid so much as to put it in any real jeopardy, not when he was young, not now either.

People liked Jake. He socialized with his fellows. He did his share. He contradicted no one.

The crop house was a vast structure supporting plastic sheets that filtered out ultraviolet radiation. It had been Jake's workplace for almost two decades. When the workday was done Jake went with the other farm workers to the communal dining hall. Saint Simon, their overseer, led them in grace. Their dishes were filled with corn mush and beans, same as always. An hour of prayer would follow.

Saint Simon approached Jake. "Saint, you are wanted by Mother Barbara."

"Thank you, Saint."

For a time, whenever he was called Saint, Jake thought "slave." But over the years, for him, the term Saint came to mean exactly what he was. A powerless survivor of the Apocalypse. The young men who worked in the fields, the resurrected ones, were not called Saints. They were called Children.

Now he was certain that somehow they, his superiors, had found him out. They pretended to represent God. One part of him always maintained they were total frauds, but another part of him had succumbed to the pressure of years of post-Apocalypse society. That part of him believed in their omnipotence if not their actual divinity.

Paranoia thrives on coincidence. After years of routine subservience he was planning to escape Zion and after years of routine supervision he was called to see Mother Barbara. In the past he had only seen her when she led prayers or made some sort of inspection. Friends had been called to her to be punished, or to disappear. Hence he figured she knew he planned to escape Zion, and was summonsing him to punishment.

He knew the way to her office. Technically he was not a prisoner, but a citizen of Zion. He needed no armed escort. Obedience was a lesson he had learned long ago. All survivors had learned that lesson.

Clearly, as if it had happened yesterday, he remembered the first time he had gone to a mission for a free meal. It was during the Great Recession, in 1995. He was sixteen and his father had lost his job as a steelworker, and his house, and most of his family. Jake had planned on ducking out of being a fourth generation steelworker anyway, he knew it was real hard work. Jake got as far as Nashville, where he used his last money to rent a room for a week. From talking to bums in his hometown he knew he could get food for free. Only the first place he tried was a church and when he had sat down he had to listen to over an hour of preaching before the meal was served. It was as bad as working, maybe worse, depending on the job.

Jake smiled his most saintly smile as his steps brought him within sight of the doorway to Mother Barbara's office. He had not been thinking of escaping, he assured himself. His life as a saint was contented. His spirit felt purified, ready for any task God might assign to its eternal life.

"Bless me, Mother Barbara," he said to her.

She was five years younger than Jake, but bore her aging much better. When prettiness had mattered, before the Apocalypse, she had been a pretty woman; as much as Jake had been a handsome man. Her face, however, displayed an animated friendliness that was neither forced nor genuine, just habitual. Seeing it he knew he was not in trouble. Something else had caused him to be summoned.

"You have done God's labor for many years," she said by way of opening.

"It is a blessing to tend to his vineyards," he said. Even though no one had seen a grape in decades. Resurrect that.

"We need someone to tend our most special crop. Someone hard working and reliable, as you have proven to be. God has granted us a special blessing, speeding up the Resurrection of the Dead.

We need more Saints to help with the Resurrection."

"I am happy to do as God wishes, Mother."

"Our most important crop, Saint, is souls. The souls of the resurrected are in some ways more delicate than yours or mine. They have been carefully nurtured in body and in spirit. In your new job you will sometimes be working with God's resurrected Children. They may ask you about the past. You must handle such questions in a manner that takes into account the developing souls of these children."

"I will not speak of the past, Mother."

"No, what we require is that you exercise care about what you say about the past. You went through a very traumatic period, did you not?"

"Yes, Mother."

"The Children must be spared of trauma. You will spend a few days in training. We will teach you the best responses to the questions the children may ask. You will be assigned a spiritual guide to help you if you have difficulty working with the children. I do not think you will find it difficult."

"I will serve God with my whole heart and soul, Mother."

"Good. You may tell your friends you are leaving to work on a different farm, no more and no less. Then you will report to the Clerk with your personal possessions. You will be sleeping with new friends tonight."

"Thank you, Mother."

"God bless you, Saint."

Chapter 4

"You will want to wear these," said Saint Mary Jones. She handed Ann a pair of sunglasses. Ann saw they were darkened versions of the reading glasses that some of the children wore. She watched Mary balance the glasses on her nose, and then imitated her.

"You have never been out in the sun, have you, Ann?" said the Saint.

"No Mother."

"You had better close your eyes at first. Even with the sunglasses the light will be too bright for you. After a minute or two your eyes will adjust and you can open them."

Ann closed her eyes.

"It is going to be noisy, too. Do not let it frighten you."

There was a roaring mechanical noise that any Saint would recognize: the starting of an automobile. Ann did not see the garage door opening, but light seeped red through her eyelid, building in intensity until she wanted to cry out in pain and amazement.

Acceleration pressed her back into the seat and she began to be bounced around. Gradually, however, the light coming through her eyelid faded to a dull red. Ann ventured to crack her left eye open, but the sight outside the window confused her: a wall in front of the car had its upper half colored blue while its lower half was shades of bright brownish yellow. Peering at it she watched vague shapes flow down it like corn mush from a spoon.

She looked at Mary, who looked straight forward, ignoring Ann. With both eyes open Ann gazed out the forward window again. Her eyes followed the line of the front hood of the car forward to where the yellow wall rushed into it. Then, instantly, the yellow wall became the ground and the blue sky became her ceiling. A sort of path through the yellow-brown lay before them. Her eyes followed it into the distance, where it became a blur.

"It is so big," she ventured, not sure if it was proper to speak to Mary except to answer a question.

"It will take all day to get to Resurrection City. We will stop to rest once or twice. There are three towns along the way: Gideon, Ruth, and Shiloh. We could stop at them, or we could stop at a river."

"I have never seen a river. I have never seen anything, except pictures."

"We will see how it goes. Maybe we will stop at Ruth and at the Providence River crossing."

"Yes, Saint Mary."

Saint Mary made a brief, strange look with her face, which Ann could not interpret, having not seen it before. Mary's eyebrows had moved toward the centerline of her face.

"That is Saint Mary Jones, Child," she said, smiling. "It is fine to call me Mary, but Saint Mary is the Mother of God. You know that, do not you?"

"Pray forgive me, Saint Mary Jones."

"Forget it."

Which was not right, Mary realized, you were supposed to say "Forgiveness is granted" to a resurrected Child of God in such circumstances. But something prevented Mary from emphasizing the mistake by correcting it. A pre-apocalyptic thought pattern. She could tell that Ann noticed the change from the established pattern, but was too deferential to adults to say anything.

Ann Swanson, Mary Jones thought, resurrected from the dead. By the Mother of God. Just as the Scriptures had promised. And now she was taking the girl to the Temple of Resurrection, to aid the Mothers in further resurrections, no doubt. They have promised, when this body is too old to go on, that they will resurrect me. The aging process had been slowed, that was an observable fact, and certainly resurrection was possible. Ann Swanson and thousands of other Children of the Mother of God were proof. And hard as life had been since the Apocalypse, Mary preferred life to death.

Mary liked to talk, despite the general admonition in New Zion that talk was to be kept to a minimum. Sometimes she found other people who did not mind talking. Ann seemed like a talker, and Mary determined to resume the conversation at some point. The landscape failed to fascinate Mary, but she knew Ann had never been outside before, and would want an eyeful.

Ann found it was easiest to see things at a distance where they moved slowly. When items of interest (usually rocks, sometimes various forms of pre-apocalyptic debris) approached the window, they became larger and seemed easier see, but only for a moment. That was called perspective, according to the schoolbooks.

White shadows appeared ahead against the blue sky.

"Are those clouds?" asked Ann.

"Yes, those are clouds. If enough of them gather today it might rain."

"I would like to see rain," said Ann.

"After you have seen it enough times, it is not so interesting. If it rains I will have to drive slower, and we will not get you to your new home until nightfall."

"Oh, I did not know that. What are all the things on the ground?"

"Well, there are lots of different things. Those small roundish things are just rocks. Most of the reddish brown things are cars or equipment from before the Apocalypse. They were made of iron, and the red is from the rusting of the iron. Up ahead to your left is the remains of an old house. Once there was a barn behind it but it fell down about five years ago."

"People lived there?"

"Yes, and when they are resurrected they will live there again."

"Why does not the Mother of God resurrect everyone all at once?"

Saint Mary Jones felt her muscles stiffen.

"Do not start why-ing me," she said, trying not to be cross. "I only know what is."

No one, Ann felt, had to answer questions except Children, and then they just repeated whatever the books or Mothers had told them.

Something shone in the distance, near the line where the blue sky met the yellow-brown earth. It grew larger very slowly.

"We are getting near one of the farms now," Mary volunteered. "The food you eat grows in that big building, or one like it. This one grows oats, which are part of the cereal you get fed."

The farm was a funny sort of white. It ran to the right as far as Ann could see. The road looked like it would go right by, but when they came very close Ann realized the distance between the farm and the road was quite large. With her eyes focussed on the farm building she was suddenly surprised when a large dark crack in the earth appeared. Turning ahead she saw they were rushing towards one of the big brown equipment things.

They went straight through it, leaving the crack in the earth behind.

"That was a bridge. That stream is called The Little Miracle. Most of the water goes to grow the plants in the farm."

"A stream is a small river," Ann recited.

"Yes, that was a small river. Much smaller than the Providence."

The road had turned black, and less bumpy. "Why is the road black?"

"It is paved with asphalt. All of the roads from here to the city are paved. There is plenty of potholes, though."

"Potholes?"

"The asphalt wears out," explained Mary, "and it makes a hole. The car bumps on them if I do not maneuver around them."

At first little had broken the monotony of the land, but buildings, both derelict and inhabited, gradually became more common. The City of Gideon, however, was mostly underground. They stopped there to refuel, which gave Mary Jones a chance to talk about how the car worked. She liked the car, though she would have preferred it when it was new, before most of the glass windows were replaced with armor. It was a 1997 Ford minivan. It had been made over to run on alcohol. They did not make new cars in Zion. There were still plenty of old ones around to resurrect.

Even the maintenance shed where they fueled up was partly underground. Other buildings appeared to be bumps in the dry landscape. Only the farms were above ground.

Ann was allowed out of the car to go to the toilet. She wanted to look at all the strange things in the maintenance shop, and to talk to the Saints who worked there, but there was no time. A glass of water was all she was allowed.

"It must have been terrible before the Apocalypse," said Ann as they left Gideon.

"Yes," said Mary Jones, "it was terrible." She remembered the green world before the bad times came. Her heart ached to tell Ann about the old days, but she could not. She could not risk her life. The girl would know only what she was taught about pre-apocalyptic earth.

In Ruth they left the car in the maintenance shed and walked along concrete halls to a small dining area. Their meal was the usual corn mush, water, and a dish of cooked kale. Ann did not like the kale, but knew it was healthy and never considered refusing to eat it. No one else was in the room when they ate; even the Saint who served them had disappeared. Before they left the Saint brought out a metal box to Mary Jones. "This is for the river," said Mary, obviously happy about it.

Before the river came a long stretch of dead trees, their long, straight trunks identifying them as having been of the pine family. Killed in the Apocalypse, Mary explained. They had green needles, like the kale they had been served at lunch, like the corn plants that gave a green tint to the farms.

The blue sky was gradually replaced by dark clouds and rain began to fall sporadically. Ann was fascinated by the process. Around her, the barren land, seemingly flat, absorbed some of the water and tilted the rest into shallow drainages. When the rain from the storm became heavy Mary Jones stopped the car on the top of a rise. "I am pretty sure there is too much water to get through down there, and the rain will not last long. We might as well sit here."

"Does it rain often?" asked Ann.

"Sure, at this time of year it rains almost every day, usually for just an hour or two. Sometimes, though, especially in the spring and fall a week or so may pass between rainstorms."

"Why does it rain so much?"

"So people will have water." Saint Mary Jones began to feel uncomfortable.

"It is a lot of water."

"Well," said Mary Jones, "we will need it when everyone is resurrected." She paused, trying to think of a safer topic. "You must have been doing well at school to get selected for this job."

"Yes, I am good at Remembrance, Biology, and History. Mother says I must work harder at Math."

And so they talked about school and Ann's "remembrances" until the rain stopped and the road in front of them had drained enough to proceed safely. Mary Jones was careful not to comment on the world before the Apocalypse. She was sure that Ann was a girl destined for trouble, not because she was bad but because she was too curious. Survival, for Saints anyway, required a faith that Mary Jones had acquired, but she knew the fate of those who had failed to gain that faith.

The sun was shining, but low in the sky, when they arrived at the Providence River. A strip of asphalt, half covered with mud, provided a dry place for them to park and sit. The river churned before them, a torrent of yellow brown mud. The landscape was devoid of green. But to Ann it looked magnificent; she could have watched the water for hours. They ate the food they had taken at Gideon. It was sandwiches made of coarse brown bread, filled with bean curd and lettuce. Ann had never tasted anything like it, but she enjoyed it. It had more taste than the mush she was accustomed to eating. Then they actually had a desert: sweetened oatmeal cookies, one each.

By then the sun was setting, and with the slow night driving it would be well into the evening before they reached Resurrection City. Saint Mary Jones talked a little bit about the City, knowing Ann would be impressed by its size and relative luxury. If it had been daylight they would have passed other cars and trucks, at rare intervals, on this road. In the night they saw occasional lights of towns and farms, and Ann saw stars for the first time. When the moon rose she watched it so intently that Mary Jones had to point out when Resurrection City appeared in the distance.

Resurrection City was dominated by a tall spire that crowned its Cathedral of Eternal Life. At the top a statue of Mary the Mother of God and Man was lit. To Ann it seemed to float in the sky. Resurrection City was a dark shadow against the moonlit land and starlit night. Above ground it was virtually windowless, and like an iceberg it lay mostly out of sight, underground.

Eventually they arrived in the garage. A Mother was waiting to escort Ann away.

The ground shook. The half dozen people in the garage gave Ann her first look at human terror. No one spoke. The Mother grabbed Ann's hand and led her through a door.

Chapter 5

Pushing a broom is easy work if you are accustomed to hard work. Jake had spent more than two decades as a farm worker; sweeping the floors of the Temple of Resurrection seemed like no work at all. He recalled, amused, that as a young man he would have considered his new assignment an odious job. Jake busied himself over twelve hours a day, not counting mandatory prayer sessions. Yet his attitude was that of a leisurely tourist. The broom swept up dust and dirt in front of him. At intervals he placed the sweepings in a bin. Meantime he scoped out the details of life in the year 2027.

The City and especially the Temple of Resurrection were very clean places. Neither the Children nor the human relics of the pre-apocalyptic era went outdoors, though the farm laborers worked in indoor fields, segregated from the rest of the populace. There were no windows open to the outside air; all air was filtered before entering. Despite that, dust and dirt did accumulate from human detritus and the gradual wearing down of cloths, furniture and paper items.

Jake began sweeping each morning in the Children's dormitories. As the Mothers roused the children each morning Jake, Mike and Berg gathered their brooms and dustbins. As soon as the children were out of the dorms the sweeping began. Jake ran his broom over the polished wood floors, by the beds linens made perfect by children as young as 4 years old. At the age of 6 most children were transferred to one of the outlying schools, but hundreds stayed in the City for their education.

Jake pushed the broom and considered his options. The plants were coming back, either because they had finally adapted to the harsh post-Apocalypse sun or because the ozone layer was repairing itself. He might escape to freedom, that was true enough. But now he had an easy job and slightly better food. He could tell he had gained some weight even in the few weeks that had passed since he began his new job. Escape into the wilderness was no longer his most idyllic thought.

After the dormitories, he swept up the dining hall where the children had eaten, then zoomed down the halls of the Mothers' administrative area. For some reason the Mothers cleaned their own residential area, or at least Jake's crew was not invited to sweep there. Their offices would be swept at night, when they were at devotions. As the Mothers went in and out of their offices he had learned to recognize their varied faces; they all knew his name and he was learning theirs.

Around eleven-thirty Jake, Mike and Berg took their lunch with other Saints from their section of the city, over a hundred in all. There was little idle conversation among the Saints, at least in such large groups. While they ate one of their member read aloud to the group from the Liturgy.

In the afternoon Jake assisted Saint Andrew Willets with reading lessons for six children. They read Liturgy. It was pretty simple stuff; drill appropriate to seven year olds.

When he was considered worthy Jake would be given more teaching hours and less janitor's work. Sweeping was easier, but the prestige of teaching appealed to him.

It was clear from interacting with the 7 year olds that the rumors he had heard were true. The children did not actually remember their past lives. They were not resurrected as their adult selves, but were born as infants and developed fairly normally, at least until they were 12 or so. Then their sexual development was arrested. All the children looked pre-pubescent to him, but some of the ones who were working in the City had to be in their twenties. His own interest in sex had declined to nothing after the Apocalypse. Well, to be more precise, after Zion was operating under the Mothers, who attributed the decreased sexuality to the divine intervention of God.

He remembered fondly the brief period of time when his semen, like all semen, was in great demand, when the women first stopped having babies. But that had not lasted long. Semen apparently had not been the problem.

Still, it was fun to interact with the Children, if only to help them read things like "Mary, the Mother of God, loves all her good Children. She promised all good Children eternal life, and the Resurrection is proof of her eternal love."

After lessons Jake swept into the Temple of the Resurrection. He did not sweep around the actual apparatus of the Resurrection, though Mike had showed him part of it once. For Jake it seemed like a pre-apocalypse science fiction movie: glass and metal in strange shapes everywhere, with computers, gauges, blinking lights, the whole schmear. He had also seen dozens of babies in incubators and cribs, but no pregnant women. "Test tube babies" was the term he remembered from his youth, but he did not ask Mike if that were true. Pregnant Mothers might be dormed someplace special he had not seen.

Jake's least favorite time of day was evening service. It was especially irritating because it came before dinner, at a time when his stomach told him he should be chowing down. When the Mother intoned the first prayer –

"We have passed through Apocalypse,
We have been purified by its fire,
We give praise to Mary the Mother of God,
We glory in the Resurrection of the dead."

– his mind went into automatic. He said the prayers with proper fervor even as his mind wandered hither and thither. He did like to sing, he always had. Yet even then his eyes wandered over the backs of his church mate's heads, thinking good or ill of them as he thought they merited it.

Dinner was seldom more than grain mush or bread and boiled vegetables. On Sundays there would be a pudding. He remembered the food was much better before the Apocalypse, even at the soup kitchens. He had to repress a laugh, thinking how he had complained about the "vegan" grub Food Not Bombs had given him in Golden Gate Park in San Francisco. He was there when the police arrested them for distributing free food. Lucky he was not in San Francisco when the Army of God swept into town.

After dinner he helped to feed the two year old children. Then he had his best time of the day: a round of cleanup at the technicians' offices of the Temple of Resurrection. Mostly he had to empty trash cans. Usually no one was working, so no one was watching him. He could take a moment to look at a piece of paper or even sit in a chair and rest a second.

By the time he was done he was late for scripture reading. After years of farm labor he had been in a rut, and the scripture had worn grooves in his mind though he was already half asleep. Now, stimulated by a new and more complex environment, he returned to his old humorous cynicism. He had been force fed the Bible before the Apocalypse, and like a monkey had learned to recite parts of it in order to please his feeders. The Scripture was not the Bible. They had even stopped using the term Christianity. God had been displaced by the Mother of God, represented on earth by Mary Mother of God. Well, for some reason the Mothers and their Saints were alive while their rivals were dead. If he had to work and pray for his food, so what, that had always been true. On earth as it is in heaven.

Chapter 6

Resurrection City was a marvel. Saint Mary Jones handed Ann over to Saint Margaret Simon in a vast chamber filled with some two dozen vehicles; it was easily twice the size of the biggest hall in her old child care facility. But the walk that followed was, in its own way, as marvelous as her trip through the Ohio desert. Saint Margaret said little, except to occasionally urge Ann to walk faster. Ann passed doorway after doorway, each marked, each, she was sure, holding mysteries. Sometimes the corridors they walked went for great distances without any doors at all. Often Saints, Mothers and Children passed by them; some, Ann was sure, by deduction, were men or boys. She would have liked to have stopped and talked to any or all of them, but usually they passed by without so much as a greeting.

It took over half an hour to walk to their destination, an amount of exercise Ann had never been exposed to before. But her body bore it well; her mind was too enchanted with the novelty to pay any attention to the complaints of her legs. The room they finally entered was labelled "Temple School Dining Hall." Inside sat hundreds of people eating. A Mother got up from her meal and walked over to them.

"Praise be to Mary," she said. "This must be Ann Swanson. Welcome, child. Thank you, Saint." and Saint Simon left them.

"Come and eat your dinner. You're late through no fault of your own." She led Ann to the serving area, which was being cleaned up. "Bring this Child a plate of food. She just came in from one of the remote child care facilities."

It did not take long for a Saint to produce a tray holding Ann's dinner. Unfortunately the food was not marvelous, being little different than what she would have received back at the child care facility. Corn mush, boiled beans, and a green salad, with a glass of water to drink. But it had never occurred to her that food could be better, so there was no cause for complaint. Mother instructed her to sit down at an empty place at a table. A moment later she returned with a somewhat older Child.

"Ann Swanson, this is Lillian Grant. Lillian will wait with you and take you to Liturgy when you have eaten. You will be sleeping in the same dorm with her, so she can take you there too."

"Mary's Grace to you, Sister Swanson," said Lillian.

"Mary's Grace to you, Sister Grant," said Ann.

But that ended their conversation, for talking during dinner was frowned upon. A bell rang and everyone else left the hall for Liturgy.

Ann hoped Lillian would initiate a conversation, but when she did not, ventured, "Have you been in Resurrection City long, Lillian?"

Lillian replied, "Long enough to devote myself to Mary Mother of God, rather than engaging in idle chatter."

Great, thought Ann, I hope everyone here is not like Lillian.

She finished off her food quickly, figuring even Liturgy would be more interesting than Lillian. After taking her tray to the disposal area she was led out of the hall.

The Hall of Worship was directly next to the dining hall. Lillian and Ann entered quietly and sat in the rear. The custom was that those who entered first sat in the first row, and each row was filled successively. They had missed the simple prayers that began each service. A Mother was reading from the Liturgy.

"By now everyone had left the General Holofernes and no one, whether important or unimportant, was left in the bed chamber. Standing beside the bed, Judith murmured to herself: God our Mother, to whom all strength belongs, prosper what my hands are now to do for the greater glory of Jerusalem. Now is the time to recover your heritage and further my designs to crush the enemy encamped about us. With that Judith went up to the bedpost by Holofernes' head and grasped his scimitar. Approaching the bed she caught him by the hair and prayed: Make me strong today, Mary

Mother of Israel. Twice she struck at his neck with all her strength and cut off his head. Then she rolled his body off the bed and tore the canopy down from the bedposts. Soon after, she went out and gave the head of Holofernes to her attendant, who put it in her food bag. The two then left the camp together, as they always did when they went to pray. Once they were out of the camp they skirted the ravine, climbed the slope to Bethulia and made to the gates.

"Then she hung the head of the Babylonian general from the wall and called upon the townspeople. Our God and Mother has granted us victory. See before you the head of Bethulia, whom only yesterday caused you to tremble at his sight. Now take up your weapons and raise a loud noise. Form a line outside our wall and approach the Babylonian army. They will run for Bethulia and find him missing, and then they will see his head hanging above our walls. They will flee before you; if any does not flee fast enough, kill him.

"The women of the town put on their armor and took up their weapons, and the men of Israel went with them, and the Grace of their God Mary went before them. And the Babylonians fled, but the Israelites caught many of them and killed them or took them for slaves. Then there was great rejoicing in Israel, for the people of one town had defeated the whole army of the Babylonians. And Judith had a temple built there in praise of God, and the people of the town of Bethulia lived out their lives in peace, for their enemies feared their God and her Priestess Judith.

"So it was in ancient Israel. But an age of Darkness fell upon the land, and Lucifer the envious male blinded men's eyes and told them to praise him as God. And even Mother Mary's son, Jesus, who she sent to redeem mankind, even his name was usurped by Lucifer, who we call Satan and the Devil. And Mary allowed this age of Darkness as a test, to separate out the good from the bad. But the Sons of Satan grew mighty, and the mightiest of all they called the Pope. And Satan called on all men to treat women as slaves, and yet many women were not broken. Many women knew that Satan ruled through the Pope and Men, and they worshipped Mary in their hearts.

"Be like Judith of ancient Israel. Do not be afraid of Satan because he raises armies and blusters about. Put your trust in our God. Only She can protect you when the day of reckoning comes. Only She can give the gift of life everlasting. Only She can raise the dead who were faithful to Her to allow them to enjoy Heaven on Earth."

"For everything is Her creation..."

Ann's mind wandered off. She liked the story of Judith, but she had heard it many times before. Instead she began wondering what the Temple of the Resurrection would be like. To think that she would work there! She would be a handmaiden to the greatest miracle of all. She was very proud to be selected. Of course she knew that she must practice humility. In fact, the Mothers had taught her that even the Child that plants the crops of the fields or washes the dishes of the dining halls is of great importance to Mary Mother of God. Each task contributes to the whole, and each task is equally important. Still, she knew that agricultural work was boring. It was work for male Children, for their brains were not usually fit for mental or supervisory work. Yet Mary loved them just the same, and granted them the gift of Resurrection.

She was eager to study and to work. Work at the child care facility had been assignments to help the Saints with cleanup or food preparation. Here it would be assisting at the Temple. Perhaps her studies would go faster too: the pace at the facility had seemed rather slow to her.

When the service was over it was time for study. For this the Children split up into different groups, each occupying a hall considerably smaller than the Hall of Worship. Since Ann did not yet have any books, Lillian lent her one. It was Geometry, a math book. Ann considered math boring, but dutifully began reading about points, lines and planes.

Again a bell rang and the Children filed off to their dorms. There were only nine girls in each dorm room, three to each of the triple-tiered bunks. A Mother came by to make sure the lights were out. Ann could tell the other girls fell right to sleep, as she normally would have. But despite her fatigue she was too excited. It was 11 P.M. and the wake up bell doubtless would ring at 5 A.M. Closing her eyes she recalled the statue of Mary the Mother of God that had watched over the city. She wanted to remember it always, and to remember the river and the road and everything she had seen that day. She might never leave Resurrection City again; but she hoped she would.

Chapter 7

Mary Kate Ashton was one of the first resurrected of the Children. In fact, she was 23rd, one of the last of 2005, and the first Child to test with intelligence significantly above normal. She had been born in 1955, on February 16th, to Walter and Jean Ellen Grue, at the Cleveland General Hospital. Her parents were good people in a Methodist Church. When she was 20 years old, in 1975, she married a fellow in her Church, Randal Ashton. In 1978 she gave birth to the first of her three children, Andrew; Terry and Jean Marie followed. In 1993 she joined the Church of Mary and Jesus, a true church founded by Mother Hilary Prophet, an emissary of Mary the Mother of Jesus. She was killed when worshippers of the Devil rioted in 1997. So she slept only 8 years before she was resurrected.

She looked forward to the day she would be reunited with her three children, her parents, and especially her husband Randal. She remembered them very clearly, and had pictures of them. Meanwhile, she worked as a gene reconstructionist in the Temple of the Resurrection, and continued her studies of embryology and cell chemistry. In a few years she hoped to be an actual Facilitator of

Resurrections, capable of supervising the entire process.

The process began with materials recovered from pre-holocaust graves. Genetic material was stored primarily in the nuclei of cells, and within the nuclei primarily in the chromosomes. The core of the chromosomes themselves consisted of strands of DNA, which had four components: adenine, guanine, cytosine and thymine. The four components were in a coded sequence, which was God's way of instructing the body how to grow and behave.

Unfortunately death caused the DNA sequences to deteriorate; depending on the cause of death and the storage environment after death the deterioration might be moderate or severe. Fortunately all human beings had almost identical genetic make ups. The variations in the DNA sequences that accounted for individuality constituted less than one percent of the DNA of any person. The Facilitators had a baseline DNA sequence stored in their computer.

Even a small amount of flesh is composed of hundreds of thousands of cells. By comparing any intact DNA from each cell to the baseline sequence the facilitators could gradually map the one percent of the DNA responsible for individuality.

They did not actually use the DNA from the dead tissue to engender the Children. Once the entire code was worked out on the computer a chemical sequencer began producing the chromosomes. This was a tricky process because the DNA had to be properly coated with protein and folded in order to be viable. The protein coat determined, for instance, whether the DNA would create a skin cell or blood cell; the goal was to create the equivalent of a fertilized ovum. Only the proper coating for an ovum would start the cell on the embryo-logical sequence that would result, ultimately, in the resurrection of a living Child.

Once an ovum was made, many things could go wrong. The only real test of an ovum's viability was whether it developed into an embryo, which in turn developed into a Child. Several ova failed for each success. One facilitator's group did nothing but monitor failures. Their work often resulted in special attention being paid to various aspects of fashioning the DNA and its coating.

As far as Mary Kate could tell the Magic Encyclopedia correctly related much of the information about DNA, chromosomes, cell structure and embryology. In fact she learned much more about cell structure from the Encyclopedia than she had from her classes. The different encyclopedias within the database varied mainly in the amount of detail they gave in describing genetics. One entry from just before the Apocalypse mentioned the Human Genome Project, which she guessed was used to create the Temple's baseline sequence. Some of the older versions of the encyclopedias, however, gave incorrect information or professed ignorance about many aspects of the chemistry of reproduction. She gathered that this knowledge was a recent acquisition of mankind. She wondered how the knowledge was gained because she had not read a description of the scientific method.

The encyclopedia mentioned evolution. She found that idea exciting and intuitively correct, but spoke to no one about it. It had never been mentioned in her classes. Perhaps there was something wrong with it. Or maybe since the old world had come to an end, evolution was no longer important.

What really bothered her about the encyclopedia was its descriptions of life before the Apocalypse. It claimed in every version that in the 1990's the world had about 5 billion people. The Mothers had not told her how many people lived before the Apocalypse, but she guessed the current population of Paradise to be about 100,000, including about 50,000 saints and about 10,000 children. Was it possible that of all the people who were alive before the Apocalypse only a tiny percentage were spared by Christ and Mother Mary, Queen of Heaven, God and Creator of the Universe? The Encyclopedia did not make people seem evil. They seemed powerful and prosperous. They built great cities. Mary Kate tried to imagine so many people refusing to do God's will. But they must have. They must have been misguided.

When she read about religion she decided it was the encyclopedia itself that misguided everyone. It did not bother her that there were many religions she had not been taught about (Buddhism, Islam, Judaism) and philosophies that seemed to reject God and religion altogether. It was the sections on Christianity and related topics that she rejected. Clearly they were written by misguided people: men, doubtless, an emotional sex virtually incapable of rational thought.

The Mothers had talked much of the male angel Lucifer and how he had misguided the followers of the Son of God, Jesus. But according to the encyclopedia most followers of Jesus, Christians they were called, thought that Jesus Christ was God, and that God the Father of Jesus was the Creator of the Universe. To them Mary was a mere human, a vessel for the birth of Jesus. In fact they invented a great deal of garbage to obscure their lack of faith and understanding, exemplified in three sentences from the Encyclopedia:

> The doctrine of Mary's bodily assumption into heaven can be traced to apocryphal documents dating from the 4th century, but this doctrine was not officially formulated and defined for Roman Catholics until 1950 (see ASSUMPTION OF MARY). The doctrine of Mary's IMMACULATE CONCEPTION was a matter of dispute throughout the Middle Ages. In 1854, however, Pope Pius IX

declared that Mary was freed from original sin by a special act of grace the moment she was conceived in the womb of Saint Anne.

Of course, Mary did not need to be bodily assumed into Heaven: as God, her intellect dwelt in Heaven, but she was the very substance of the Universe. It was her decision to manifest herself on earth in order to give birth to Jesus and hence to a male redeemer that should have been of interest to the encyclopaedists. The idea that only 50 years before the Apocalypse, 1970 years after Mary first appeared in material form on earth, the Roman Catholics declared that she was assumed bodily into heaven, was absurd.

She wanted to learn more, however, about the religions that men had strayed into. What she had read so far in the encyclopedia had been difficult to understand, and meant little to her. She had a list of sects she had not yet read about. For instance, the article on Mother Mary mentioned Roman Catholics, Anglicans, and Protestants. She had yet to look them up.

She thought that perhaps the Mothers had only hinted at the evil of men. The encyclopedia indicated, by way of use of male names, that men were prominent in the pre-apocalyptic society. Perhaps they even wrote the encyclopedias. They felt, perhaps, a need to elevate Jesus Christ to godhood. Yes, that would explain much. But would Mother Mary punish billions of people just for mistaking her son, a mere messenger, for a God?

That hardly seemed just. It must have been the actual bad deeds of the men misguided by Lucifer. Mary wished she could ask the Mothers questions, as well as the encyclopedia. But she knew that the Mothers did not like to be asked questions. Not at all.

Increasingly Mary Kate worked late into the night, even when she was not required to do so. Partly she wanted to learn her biology all the quicker. She certainly preferred that to prayers or other chores. But often she looked at the Magic Encyclopedia.

Because she worked late she frequently saw Jake. Yet they had not talked beyond the common greeting that was allowed. She had been considering this Saint, in his maleness, as a possible source of the evil that existed before the Apocalypse. But she knew he did not serve as a good example: after all, he had survived the Apocalypse, so he must have been in Mary's graces. Still, like all males, Saints and Children alike, he was consigned to physical labor, indicating that a danger, a potential for evil, lurked in him.

One evening when he came in to clean up and discovered her there, after saying "Greetings, Child of God," he ventured, not for the first time, to say "Working late again, I see."

And she decided to respond. To have a conversation with a male. But carefully, at first. "I enjoy it, studying biology and helping in the Resurrection."

He was startled. He made a point of continuing his work as he said, "even my humble work cleaning here helps in the Resurrection. I hope to please Mary."

And that would have been the end of the conversation, had he not knocked over a trash can. For a moment, as the metal reverberated against the floor, he was paralysed.

"Earthquake," he said. A part of his mind screamed "No, Danger, No!" but it was too late.

Silence.

Mary Kate spoke: "Earthquake."

Jake cursed himself silently.

Mary Kate almost turned to her work, then asked again: "Earthquake. What does that mean?"

The old man, the Saint, looked at the floor.

The social relations between Saints and Children were unclear. Both were clearly under the order of the Mothers. In theory the Saints were the privileged survivors of the holocaust, but in reality everyone's attention centered on the Children.

Jake considered. He was not supposed to talk to the children about the past. Was a word, defining an event, part of the past?

"That is fine," said Mary Kate. "I can ask Mother Anne Marie what it means."

"Shit," that was the old, now-banned word that screamed in Jake's head.

"I am surprised you do not know," intimated Jake. "The earth shakes sometimes. Not often. Mostly you cannot feel it. Sometimes you can. In a bad earthquake, a strong one, things get knocked over. A trash can, some dishes from a shelf. In a real bad earthquake sometimes whole buildings fall over."

"I see. Thank you."

"You are welcome. I should finish my work."

"Certainly. What is your name?"

"Jake, Jake Thompson."

"My name is Mary Kate Ashton. And I have one more question. Was there an earthquake, the kind you can feel, recently?"

"No, we are in the mid-west. They happen pretty often on the west coast of the continent. But there was one here around the time of the Apocalypse."

"So earthquakes are bad."

"I have never heard anyone say anything good about them," admitted Jake.

Mary Kate turned to her work. Jake hurried his cleanup and exited.

Chapter 8

Ann's head swam, something her body had never done, and a stranger experience still because of it.

She had imagined the resurrection of the dead as a sort of miracle. In fact, she had been told over and over again that it was a miracle. A miracle that, before the Apocalypse, had occurred only on a few occasions, most notably when Mary the Mother of God caused her son Jesus to rise from the dead after he was crucified.

Ann had died of the plague in 1998. It had been a horrible death, as all deaths from the plague had been. She had worked at the Methodist hospital in Knoxville, Tennessee, a vast building filled with the sick and their attendants. The plague attacked the good and bad alike, for it was a test and a warning of the Apocalypse about to come. They lay in their beds, fevered, denying that it was the plague and that it would kill them. No disease germ had been discovered to explain the plague; no method of transmission had been deduced; no treatment slowed its course. A few lucky people turned out to have some more ordinary cause for their fever; the same people might return only a week or two later with a new fever, the plague fever. The fever never left as the plague burned the body to waste and tortured the soul like the devil on earth. While they had the strength people screamed; pain killers availed not, for only a lethal dose would quiet the wretched sinners. This might last days or even weeks, until the victims brain turned to jelly and pushed out the dead eyeballs.

It was a nightmare, a nightmare she remembered having as a child. Her mother would wake her, telling her it was just a dream. But in 1998, day after day, she went to the hospital. She fed those who could be fed, gave experimental medications to the dying, and helped remove the corpses. Her fellow nurses and the doctors died with the same frequency as the rest of the world's people: exposure to the diseased did not seem to increase a person's chances of contracting it. Neither was it possible to hide from it.

Finally her turn came: the fever set in. She was sure she had gained immunity to the disease a year earlier, when it took its first victims. But it was not a normal disease, not the normal course of nature. It was a test, and she was tested, as was the faith of the living who endured that mere prelude to the grander, final war between good and evil that lay a mere two years in the future. She lay down with the fever only when she no longer had the strength to bathe and feed her wretched charges. She prayed to God, Mother Mary, but to no avail, just as she had seen people pray to their Gods. But she never cursed as many cursed.

When the darkness of death came it was a relief.

Someone must have pulled her putrefying body out of its bed to be hauled to the grave. Then her body lay safely in the earth through the terror and glory of the Apocalypse.

Mary the Mother of God fulfilled her promise, and in Resurrection City, in Paradise, the New Zion, Ann Swanson's body was restored to life. She was a Child of Mary, cared for by the Mothers and the Saints. She would live forever. Her sisters would live forever, and so would her brothers. Everything was perfect in Paradise.

Except that her body, when she died, had been an adult body. And when she had been resurrected it had been an infant's body, perhaps even a baby's body.

And so it had been grown. Resurrected from genetic material.

Which was a miracle of sorts. But she had imagined a corpse (she had never seen a real corpse since her resurrection, only pictures in her instruction books) lying ugly and inanimate on the altar, and a Mother Superior standing over it with her attendants, praying for and witnessing the gift of God, the flesh, mind, and soul suddenly restored, and the Sinner reborn and welcomed to paradise, the resurrection of the dead, life without end, forever and ever, amen.

But of course she should have known better. In her earliest memories she was tiny, and she must have been resurrected for three or four years. The older children were bigger, and she got bigger too.

She had not remembered much at first. Strange. You might think that the memory of an event, or of a lifetime, would be strongest at first and then gradually fade. As memories did for her now.

So she had pieced it together before they actually laid it out. Here we have the genetic material, in the chromosomes, in the nucleus. There we have the computers, reconstructing DNA codes, for they had been damaged by death. Here we have the code unravelling in the marvel of embryology. There are the rows of glass wombs and the great machines that maintain them. Here we have the resurrection of the dead. There, there is a baby, hungry, beautiful, waiting to be fed and then educated.

There had been a corpse, the corpse of Ann Swanson, the corpse of a nurse who had been a faithful worshipper of Mother Mary, but who was stuck down by the Great Plague.

The nurse had had a soul, a mind, a personality.

The corpse had none.

And Ann Swanson, walking from blood donor to blood donor, watching the privileged Mothers and Saints give their precious bodily fluids, monitoring them, making sure they did not bleed to death, making sure the machines were working and performing their share of the great miracle, the great circle, the resurrection of the dead; she had a soul, a mind, and a personality. She had memories, both of her life as a resurrected Child, and as a dweller in that strange land, that terrible place, the world before the Apocalypse.

But they had never, she suspected, told her how it was done, back at Womb of Mary VII. It was her own silliness, perhaps: why call them Children if they were resurrected from adults? Well, of course we are all the children of our Mother.

In the west wing lay a great refrigerator. Her corpse had been brought there, as all the corpses of the Children were brought there. They had taken samples. They had analyzed the samples. They had made her.

They were merely the instruments of God. This was just how God preferred to resurrect the dead. She could hardly be expected to supervise the day to day activities.

They could have made two of her. And if they had, which would get her old soul? Perhaps souls could be duplicated, like DNA or the cells of the body.

But they had told her: once the baby is made, they cremate the body. The genetic code is kept in the computer.

As far as she could tell, Ann Swanson could look forward to living forever.

"I wonder what it will be like to live forever," said Ann to Jake when he came by with his broom.

"It is hard to imagine," said Jake, who continued his sweeping, leaving Ann behind.

"How long have you been alive?" she said, hoping to keep him from leaving. She liked Jake. You were supposed to like everyone, but not one particular Saint or Mother or Child, but she liked Jake. They talked sometimes. Jake was very helpful, everyone said so. Once Jake had helped her when a tube sprang a leak, almost resulting in the loss of a child. And he had told her it was okay to ask Kate questions, if she needed help.

"I am about forty-eight years old. I was born in 1979, on the old calendar."

"You could have met me before the Apocalypse. I did not die until almost the end of 1998."

"1998 was a very bad year. Everyone knows that."

"Things are so much better now, now that Mary has defeated Satan. You must be glad you lived through those evil times. Of course, if you died you would probably have been resurrected."

Jake just looked at her, as if he wanted to say something, and instead turned to his sweeping, saying "Mary willing, I will see you tomorrow."

Ann had only known Kate a few weeks, but they had become confidants. Kate was teaching Ann about gene reconstruction, just as the Mothers taught her about other aspects of work in the Temple. But she felt more on a level with Kate, more able to ask questions and talk about things, when they had the occasion to be alone.

The next day she said to Kate, "I got the distinct feeling that Jake's silence meant that he disagreed. Either he thinks he would not have been resurrected, or that things were better before the Apocalypse. I am sure the Apocalypse itself was terrible, but surely it was worth it to cleanse the earth of sin and usher in the reign of Mary."

Kate said nothing.

"I am beginning to think," said Ann, "that a number of things the Mothers taught me may not be true."

"I think," said Kate, "that a number of people think that, especially the Saints. What is the difference between a Saint and a Mother? Did you ever think of that? Do not ever say I said this, but I think the Saints agree with the Mothers out of fear. The Mothers will cast them out of Zion if they disagree. They know what really happened before we were resurrected, but they tell the stories the Mothers have told them to tell. I should not have told you this, but I am tired of being alone, unable to talk to anyone. You will not tell anyone, will you?"

"No. I will not tell. But I want to know the truth."

"Perhaps in time someone will trust us enough to tell us. In the meantime, learn what you can."

Chapter 9

Within the group now known as the Mothers there had been two great power struggles. But the Mothers were a conglomerate of many groupings that had existed before the Apocalypse, and to truly understand them you would have to understand each of those groups and their contributions to the post-apocalyptic order.

The 1990's were turbulent years, as you might expect the years before the Apocalypse to be. The disarray occurred at every level of society, in every economic class, and in every facet of culture, from art to religion to politics. Many people clung to ancient belief systems that gave them a sense of stability in a rapidly disintegrating world. At the same time hundreds of new religious, cultural and political sects emerged around the world. But this was only the final acceleration of the trend was as old as civilization.

The Church of Mary and Jesus was founded by Mother Hilary Prophet who claimed to be an emissary of Mary the Mother of Jesus. While some critics accused her of being a charlatan more interested in money and power than in truth, only fools denied the appeal of her innovations, and she had many imitators. She had been raised Catholic, then revolted and became first an atheist and then a feminist Pagan. But most traditional women rejected paganism, even though they might be attracted to a female-centered religion. The Catholic Church, a thoroughly patriarchal organization, was actually growing rapidly in the United States of America partly because it encouraged women to pray to Mary the Mother of Jesus, who was portrayed as immortal, but not herself a god.

Hilary Prophet taught that Mary was, in fact, herself the Supreme Deity, the creator of the Universe, and had appeared to Hilary and told her to organize the new church. Hilary taught that Mary, as part of her plan, had allowed the false male god, Satan, to appear on earth to subjugate women. Women were subjugated because they shared with Mary the ability to procreate, and had fancied that they were themselves gods who should be worshipped by their descendants. After allowing the male gods to use men to subjugate women, Mary took human form and gave birth to a son, Jesus, to redeem men from the male false gods. She showed he was her son by raising him from the dead, and she promised all men and women that followed her and her son that they would be granted immortality once the false gods were defeated.

Hilary proclaimed that after 2000 years of struggle between Jesus and the forces of evil, Jesus was victorious and Mary would soon return to earth for her final victory.

Proselytizing came easy to Hilary, who quickly recruited many of the most active female priests and ministers from the traditional Christian sects. Her Church of Mary and Jesus was modelled administratively after the Catholic Church, and she was declared its first High Priestess, and then its Pope (and got great publicity, being called the "femalc Pope" by the sensational news media).

A stern moral code, prohibiting most sexuality, was one of the responses of religious sects to those dark years; and the opposite was true too, for the impending disaster could not arrest the basic drive to experience pleasure. Sects prohibiting sexuality were too numerous to mention, but included the two largest organized religions, the Catholics and Baptists, as well as the Church of Jesus and Mary.

The most fanatical and interesting of the new strict moralists was, however, The Church of Immanation. Its founder, like Hilary Prophet, had had an unusual history. His birth name was Robert Zidavek, and his parents were atheist Communists of Jewish heritage. As a youth he was attracted to mysticism and apparently joined a number of both New Age and traditional esoteric sects. Eventually he became a Sufi, which is a designation for Islamic religious cults, often with mystical overtones. In 1984, after the death of a predecessor calling himself "Imman Bab," Robert became the leader of a tiny sect located on a farm in Arkansas, and changed his name to Bab Tafsir. He became fascinated with technology and de-emphasized traditional Islam while becoming increasingly in favor of celibacy — for the other men in his group.

A technology called virtual reality, which was an extension of television and computers, was used by Bab to convince novices of the correctness of his visions. He taught that biological life on earth would die, but that his followers would live forever in a heaven created by powerful computers. In the 1990's his cult spread rapidly, and his preaching against sexuality became widely known. His followers even began having medical operations to remove the glands that create sex hormones; he said this was necessary as a preparation for entering heaven. Eventually he made it a requirement for employment in his rapidly expanding business empire.

At the other end of the spectrum emerged the Church of Isis, allegedly a revival of the ancient Egyptian cult of Osiris and Isis. A rock and roll singer turned movie star, Liz Swanson, emerged as the cult's goddess and claimed to have miraculous powers, as well as to being an illegitimate descendant of an earlier goddess of the screen, Gloria Swanson. Her miraculous powers included the ability to prevent aging both in herself and in others, the ability to heal certain types of illness including AIDS, and the ability to appear to others in dreams. Part of the Church's prescription for health included an orgasm a day, minimum. In common with Hilary Prophet's Church of Jesus and Mary was the supremacy of the feminine deity. The

Church of Isis believed that the demi-goddess Isis was a manifestation of Isis the Earth Mother, which was in turn a manifestation of Isis the Universal Mother and Creative Impulse. Men could be expelled from the Church for striking a woman, and penalties for derogating women were severe. Nevertheless the sexual promiscuity encouraged by the Church resulted in no shortage of male members.

Unlike AIDS, the Great Plague of 1998 that served as a prelude to the Apocalypse was not sexually transmitted. Most religions took the same basic tact: the plague was sent by God to scourge the faithless, and joining their religion would serve as protection. It quickly became apparent that the disease struck almost completely randomly, striking the faithless as well as those of each faith with the same ferocity. Then the common line was that those who died, in one's own religion, were really lacking in faith or had somehow committed an unforgivable sin.

Bab Tafsir, Hilary Prophet, and Liz Swanson all died of the plague. In each case the death was hidden from the faithful until the Apocalypse made individual deaths a moot point.

The Church of Mary, Mother of God emerged out of the Chaos called the Apocalypse in the year 2002. By that time the population of the United States of America had dropped to about 20 million living souls; most of the rest of the world was in a similar state. The church probably never had more than a few hundred thousand members. They were mostly women with children, and they had been happy enough to see the U.S. government collapse in 2001. They formed communities mainly in the midwestern states, abandoning the large cities for small towns, and engaging in agriculture for survival.

The Church of Mary became a more radical version of the Church of Mary and Jesus, but it was initially based on the consensus faith of those who would come to be known as the Mothers, for the hierarchy of the Church of Jesus and Mary was in disarray. They believed that the Apocalypse had been brought on by men's faith in the Christian Bible, and hence banned the Bible. But they took many stories from it and adapted them, and wove many strands of faith into their consensus. Hilary Prophet and Liz Swanson were woven together, partly because Liz's daughter Isisa had survived and joined the Mothers.

The first great struggle within the Church occurred in 2005. Before then ozone layer depletion had combined with an assortment of other ecological deteriorations and civil warfare to make the growth of plants, including food crops, extremely difficult. A Children's plague killed almost everyone under the age of eight, and the Mothers realized that they had become sterile. A small scale nuclear war had taken place, the last legacy of an insane male global culture.

Though it was couched in religious terms, the struggle was over the issue of technology, and coincided with the pursuit of power by two opposing camps within the Mothers. The radical party wanted to attempt to destroy all remaining technology, but argued for this based on the supremacy of Mary the Creator of Heaven and Earth, who had allowed technology only during the recently ended reign of Men. The pragmatic party saw that abandoning technology would result in the quick extermination of the few Saints who were left. In addition they succeeded in their first resurrections that year, which appealed to the maternal, life-enhancing instincts of the majority of the Mothers. Theologically, however, the pragmatists insisted that the Apocalypse marked the dawn of the New Age in which Mother Mary would turn even male technology to good ends.

Of course, even after the Apocalypse most survivors preferred eating to starvation, and the pragmatists were able to produce food under great plastic sheets that allowed in the sunlight needed for photosynthesis but not the burning ultraviolet. The radicals wandered out into the desert; those who did not wander back, died.

The second power struggle occurred in 2012 and was more subtle. By then the Mothers Superior had created a working hierarchy that terminated in the oligarchical Council of Mary. It had gradually clarified the theology of New Zion, a theology that was universally promulgated and which allowed no open deviation. It had worked out its method for reviving the souls of the deceased as well as their bodies. However, younger Mothers who had taken over critical functions in New Zion were becoming resentful and envious of the Council of Mary's power and privileges.

Most Council members had been born in the 1950's and to a lesser extent in the 1960's. They were thus typically 60 years old, but like everyone they had been through a lot during the Apocalypse. Many required extensive medical care to keep them alive. Technical advances in medicine had continued, including several breakthroughs in preventing aging and regenerating damaged organs. So it looked as if the Council would stay alive and in power for ever, something the Mothers who were 30 to 40 years old saw as unfair. It was also true that the younger Mothers tended more towards zealotry than the older Mothers, who took their own myth making seriously but not gullibly.

Mother Jennifer Gray announced that Mary, God, had appeared to her and commanded that all of the Saints, including the Mothers, be allowed to die and then resurrected into heavenly bodies, just as the Children had been. She announced this to her friends, and added that Mary had warned her that the Council, tainted by pride, would refuse to obey Mary. A few zealots prepared to murder the Council, but the revolt frayed quickly around the edges. Very few Mothers thought that dying and being resurrected was a good way to overthrow the Council.

Mother Jennifer Gray died, as did her closest followers, but in 2027 they had still not been resurrected. Only about a dozen Mothers had died from disease or accident and been resurrected, and not a single male or female Saint had been so privileged.

Since Mary Kate was among the first to be resurrected, in 2005, she knew nothing about the two power struggles among the Mothers. To her the Mothers were God's representatives on earth, to be loved and obeyed. She did not feel threatened by them, though she had learned to automatically suppress any impulse to question or disobey them. Having advanced rapidly in the Science of Resurrection, she was treated as a friend and colleague by several of them.

It was not unusual to be called into conference with a Mother Superior, or even Council Member Tanya Jeane, who presided over the laboratories of the Temple of Resurrection. When Kate received a summons to the office of Council Member Gloria Anne, however, she was curious and apprehensive. She reasoned that it could not be because of the Magic Encyclopedia, otherwise she would have been denied access to it. So it had to be some sort of task, one outside of her scientific duties.

Gloria Anne was one of the youngest council members. She had been admitted to replace one of the two members who had been killed by Jennifer

Gray's followers. Her hair was dark brown, almost black, but well-streaked with grey. She had a rather large nose and broad forehead; combined with her almost constant smile, these features made her face mildly comical. It was almost as if the Apocalypse had not touched her, or as if she really thought she had gained paradise.

"I am very pleased to meet you," Gloria said.

"Yes, Mother," Mary Kate replied, carefully.

"There is no need to 'Yes, Mother' me," Gloria said, crinkling her face. "I am your superior, but as your superior I need to know your thoughts. I do not know everything, that is why I ask you questions. And if you have a question you think I can answer, or even if you just think I should know about it, then you should ask it." Gloria watched Kate suppress a "Yes, Mother", then continued. "Ask me why something is the way it is."

Mary Kate immediately steered her thoughts in a technical direction. "Where do the ova we use come from? They are denucleated, and mitochondria free, so how were they produced?"

Gloria laughed. "You are a good scientist. I do not know the answer. You know much more about biology than I do, though I know the basics. My specialty is educating the resurrected. I imagine Tanya Jeane can tell you, but you do not usually ask her questions, do you? I want you to ask her who to ask when you have technical questions like that. When you leave here go to her office and say you have a message from me. Now ask me a non-technical question."

Kate wanted to trust Gloria, but could not so quickly after a lifetime of caution. She could not ask if what the Magic Encyclopedia said was true. "Why did you ask me to come here?"

"Very good! Hits the nail on the head. I asked you to come here because we are resurrecting a lot of Children these days and we have a finite number of Mothers and Saints to go around. Many Children already do work, but most of it is the less mentally demanding work. Cleaning, helping with growing and cooking food, that sort of thing. Some Children, like you, are being trained for more demanding jobs, like working in the labs and even becoming scientists. But eventually some of you will be required to do more than that. You are a candidate for more general responsibilities. And more general responsibilities require a wider field of knowledge.

"After resurrecting the dead the second most important task in our society is raising the Children. That is something I want you to learn about. You will learn it by doing it. I have arranged with Tanya to have you for four hours a day. From eight to noon. Starting tomorrow. You will assist with a class of two year olds for two weeks, then rotate to a class of three year olds and so on until you have seen all the classes up to the sixteen year olds. After that you will work in record reconstruction for a few months. Probably then you will return to the Temple. The important thing is that you see what we are doing with the raw material. Would you like that?"

"Like? I will do as Mary the Mother of God wills."

"Do not we all. It is what is called a rhetorical question, a question that is really not a question but a statement. You are a smart girl. Ask smart questions. And be smart who you ask them to. A lot of questions are best answered in your own mind or by praying to Mother Mary. That is just a confirmation of what you obviously have already figured out."

"Thank you, Mother Gloria Anne."

"You can go now. We will talk again sometime. Perhaps you can tell me more about the work you do in the Temple. Bye."

"Bye."

Chapter 10

"Someone may ask, 'How are dead people raised, and what sort of body do they have when they come back?' These are stupid questions. Whatever you sow in the ground has to die before it is given new life, and the thing that you sow is not what is going to come; you sow a bare grain, say of wheat or something like that, and then God gives it the sort of body that He has chosen: each sort of seed gets its own sort of body."

— 1 Corinthians 15, 35-38

Mother Claudia Eugenius was assistant to the head of the computer department. Among her duties was security: making sure that the computers were used properly and that no one had access to information they did not need.

But Claudia was not sure about her role in rewriting history. She was not sure that it was good to tell the Children that Mary Mother of God descended with Jesus from heaven during the Apocalypse, saving the Mothers and Saints of Zion and establishing the Resurrection of the Dead. Once she had been sure. They had a rare historical opportunity: the chance to wipe the slate clean and begin all over again. To begin with a matriarchy and abolish all but the memory of a patriarchy. To bring up children free of sin. And to create a faith not seen since Europe in the Middle Ages: a confirmed faith in the existence of God, a God who cared enough to come to earth and save them from calamity.

The problem was exactly that: Mary had not come to earth. True, certain people had visions, and they were not to be discounted. But they had told the Children that Mary had come to earth, not that she had appeared in visions. Except for those who were exceptionally easily brainwashed, every Saint and every Mother knew the truth. Which meant sooner or later a Child would find out. In fact, it was likely that quite a few Children knew. She hoped so.

For instance, there was the existence of the Magic Encyclopedia. It was one of the few databases on line that was not directly related to the actual needs of Zion. She had put it on line early in the development of the current system to use for tests. It did have much useful technological information in it, but in most cases it was rather vague; more detailed and useful texts were available. Most importantly, it directly contradicted history as taught in Zion, including the history of religion.

She remembered having read *1984* in high school and seeing the movie. It was 1989 when she read it, and the following year the Evil Empire of the Soviet Union had been dismantled. She earned an associate degree in computer science at junior college, moved in with her boyfriend who was a copier technician, and figured the world was going her way. *1984* was a possibility that had not happened. Her thoughts were occasionally disturbed by stories about global warming or the cutting of the rainforests, but mainly she concentrated on her career, her relationship, and being entertained.

It was funny because there was so much in common between now and then. If she were a man she might be out in the fields pulling weeds, but she was working with computers just like in the 1990's. The food was worse, entertainment was sparse, and her boyfriend was long dead, but she had made those adjustments easily enough. Men had been evil, and the fact that most of them perished was only right. But most women had perished too, and those that remained had put on a religious straightjacket that made the corsets of the patriarchal past seem like the wings of freedom.

For entertainment she plotted the liberalization of the regime. She envisioned something like what might have happened if the Church of Mary Immaculate had triumphed instead of the Church of Mary and Jesus. Not that she had joined either Church. By a series of events or miracles she had found herself alive in the territory controlled by the Church of Mary. She had decided to keep her mouth shut, go along, and do her best to keep their computer systems up and running. Just as she had under the patriarchy, thinking that loyalty would bring her close enough to the top to satisfy her own ambition.

Claudia did not have a plan for revolution or even reform in the sense of a causal path down which people would march to victory. Rather she had decided to keep information alive and accessible. She had not been well read in the year 2000, knowing little of history beyond what she had been taught in high school (practically nothing). Since then, though her time was quite restricted, she had gradually read what was available in the encyclopedias. There had been Dark Ages before, not just the period after the fall of the Western Roman Empire. But some of the knowledge of the past was always preserved. Sometimes it was quite difficult to inject knowledge back into society; during the Middle Ages in Europe it could cost you your head. But just as humans have a desire for ignorance and superstition, they also have curiosity and a desire for truth. If the information is there, they will find it.

It was Claudia's job to report misuse of the computer system. She did that, though it did not happen often. To her superior, Mother Joseph Ann, Claudia seemed fanatically strict. This was because she reported the slightest transgressions. That allowed her, in turn, to overlook more serious transgressions when they seemed in the interest of knowledge. For instance, she knew that Mary Kate Ashton was accessing the Encyclopedia.

Claudia, in fact, had become quite a scholar. Some day she hoped to lead expeditions to recover the great libraries that had been America's true jewels before the Apocalypse. She knew that many had been burned by the Army of God and other fanatics, but doubtless many books had survived. If they were recovered the entirety of pre-apocalyptic knowledge might be reconstructed.

In the meantime her real job was to help Zion to prosper. The more it prospered, the less pressure there would be on each person. The larger the population, the harder it would be to keep it all under control. And the more time that passed, the more likely the earth would be able to heal itself. The Virgin Mary, an almighty but personal God, might be a creation of the minds of the mothers, but the Earth, which engendered all of them, was undeniably real. When the earth healed it would be possible to walk right out of Zion and start a new society based on whatever principles you liked. Maybe she would do just that.

Then there were the Mexicans. Unfortunately though her monitoring of the computers informed her of their existence and of the existence of a report on their society, the report itself had never been put on line. Apparently the Mexicans were considered potentially hostile. Did that mean that they were a Satan worshipping patriarchal society, or just that they were unlikely to let the Mothers dominate them without a fight? Claudia was dying of curiosity, and hoped that sooner or later more information would surface.

She stood up, stretching, looking around the office. She had worked through Liturgy, something that if she did too often would mark her for suspicion. Be careful, she reminded herself. Create no suspicion. Obey all conventions. If you give them control over your dress and your mouth, they will leave you control over your mind. Only they are me. They are just as afraid of me as I am of then. How many people think the same thoughts as me? Probably not enough. Not yet.

Chapter 11

"Leandra was born in 1945 in Youngstown, Ohio. Her full name was Leandra Johnston."

"Did she have a family name?" asked Timothy.

"Johnston was her family name. She did not have a middle name. Sometimes people had no middle name, and sometimes people even had two middle names. Now Leandra, what was your family name?"

"Johnston," stated the three year old girl.

"Very good, Leandra Johnston. And your mother's name was Alice Johnston. Can you say that name? Alice Johnston."

"Alice Johnston," repeated the little girl.

"Here is a picture of your mother." Mother Claire showed Leandra, then showed the other children and Mary Kate.

"You can remember your mother, you can do that, Leandra. She looked just like this picture, did she not?"

"Yes," agreed Leandra. Mary Kate could see some resemblance between the two faces: the dark skin, brown eyes, and the way the angle of the forehead led into the cheeks.

"Now David, do you remember where you were born?"

"Youngstown," said David.

"No, that is not right David, it was Leandra who was born in Youngstown. You were born in Pittsburgh. Do you remember?"

"Pittsburk," said David.

Claire smiled, knowing David would forget again, that he seemed slower than the other Children, but that he was trying, and with effort the memories would come. "Good, David. And your full name was David Stoval. Sto-val."

"Sto-val," said David carefully.

Mary Kate loved working with the children, and at first was preoccupied with doing her duty. The two year olds were played with; no one attempted to revive their memories. Now almost done with the three year olds, however, Kate began to wonder, at night when she was not preoccupied, about the system. It was obvious the three year olds remembered nothing from their previous lives. They could talk fine and most would learn the basic outlines of their pasts by the time they were four, according to Mother Claire and the other teachers.

The teachers received files on each of their charges. They included pictures of the Children as adults before the apocalypse, pictures of their parents, sometimes of siblings, and basic biographical information. In turn the Mothers wrote reports on the children's growing memories. If the child remembered a color of a house she lived in, then the Mother would write that down. If the child remembered some incident with the parents, that too went in the record.

Mary Kate had to wonder whether she was of much use in this process. With the two year olds she had reduced the loads of the Mothers and their helper Saints. With the three year olds sometimes she helped with simple drills or games, but she only watched during Remembrance.

After two weeks of three year olds Kate reported to the class of four year olds. The change was dramatic. Each Mother dealt with a half dozen children. The children knew about the Apocalypse and treated their deaths and resurrections as a matter of fact. Kate could not remember being three years old: she remembered a period of darkness, and of being four or five and knowing that she had died and now lived again. The children seemed to enjoy remembrance more than learning the alphabet or playing games. They rattled on about their previous lives. Each possessed a simple picture book about their past that the teachers had been given. Kate entered a new phase of thought: perhaps the trauma of death and resurrection just did require a period of readjustment. Maybe the four year old's memories were real.

Two days before Kate was to graduate to helping with the five year olds one of the four year olds, John Jefferson, a dark skinned, dark eyed child with a good memory, told them about his house.

"Oh, I remember my home. It was red and I lived in it with my family. My mother Rosanna, my father Walter, my older brother Walter Junior, and my three baby sisters Darlene, Tanya and Carla. Our beds were painted blue, and we all lived in the same room. It was part of a big building with lots of people in it. I played with the other children. We never went outside because there were bad men outside because Mother Mary had not come to earth to save us from the bad men. We had cereal to eat and then we would do Remembrance. In Remembrance I would remember the life I had before I died the time before. Then ..."

"John, that is a very good try, but no one did remembrance before the Apocalypse. You only lived once before the apocalypse, so you would not have any Remembrance times. Your family probably spent time praying, because you were from a good family. All of you are from good families. Now you remember that some of the prayers back then were not very good prayers because people had been misled by false religions. But it is still okay to remember those prayers, because people meant them to be good. Maybe if we say one of those prayers together that will help you remember."

"Yes, Mother," chimed the children.

Kate wished John had been allowed to go on. Maybe he had previous lives; the idea intrigued her. Maybe he would have described something that had not been pumped into him. She wondered what the inside of the buildings had looked like before the Apocalypse. Perhaps the encyclopedia would tell her. But then she was not sure she could trust the encyclopedia.

Two days after she started with the five year olds she got sick. Her head ached and her stomach rebelled. When she reported to the infirmary Mother Linda Reeves could find nothing wrong with her and suggested rest and prayer.

Chapter 12

Before the Apocalypse many people would have considered Jake an ignorant man. For no clear reason the boundaries that parents, teachers, and society tried to set for children had no effect on Jake. He began playing hookey in kindergarten. When he was physically in the classroom he was usually mentally elsewhere. Fortunately he was of average intelligence and therefore not only managed to learn the rudiments of reading, writing and arithmetic in the short spans he did allow for such matters; he actually learned enough to progress from grade to grade until the second year of high school, at which point he dropped out entirely.

Jake was not initially inclined to critical thought. He preferred experience: the feeling of his feet on a skateboard, the thrill of high speeds, the lazy good sensation of laying in the sun, swimming in music, getting off on his own neural-synaptic beat and the melodies of caffeine, alcohol, marijuana and the occasional odd pill offered by an acquaintance. His opinions were simple: I like it or I do not like it. On politics and religion he had no opinions.

He slid. As long as his parents fed him he could afford to slide. He was gifted with a good nature: he did not argue or purposefully cause trouble for his elders. They learned to expect little from him, they even found his company enjoyable. Yet the same year that he dropped out of school he left home. He had gradually spent less time there, and when an older woman (age 19, she seemed the height of sophistication to him) asked him to drive to Seattle with her, he forgot to tell his parents.

His wisdom in those early years was the wisdom of his good nature, his intuition of human character and its relation to his slide, and the massively parallel happiness of physical sensation. He gathered bits and pieces of information secondhand, just talking to people. He talked to Moonies and Mormons, Anarchists and Anabaptists, Cashiers and Cowboys, Nerds and Nihilists with varying degrees of interest. Women in particular interested him, and he interested them, so that he learned a great deal about women and their concerns.

A college educated person would have called him ignorant, because he had not read Moby Dick or The Grapes of Wrath, had not mastered Algebra much less Calculus, and could not tell you in what century Marie Antoinette lost her head. But in the 1990's, as the world slid towards disaster, a college education did not prove to be a weapon of choice in the struggle for survival. It provided no protection against the plague, or the crumbling economy, or the gradual diminishment, by use and falling production, of the world's supply of bullets.

He watched the Apocalypse with fascination and matured rapidly into a philosopher. His own life became increasingly difficult, to be sure; he actually began to do tasks for other people in return for food and shelter, sometimes even for actual cash money before that became worthless. To some extent he even enjoyed pushing a broom, carrying a load, or pounding a nail. Still, within the possibilities presented to him, he always took the easiest path. It was just that the path that was lit by the light of experience began to stretch a bit further in front of him, stretching from the needs of the moment onto a week, two weeks, even months.

Adaptation is the key to survival in a rapidly changing world. He learned the rudiments of Christianity and then Maryism in soup kitchens. Eventually he became a Saint, a cohort of the Mothers. True, he was little better than a slave, but then the world was not the luxurious world of his youth. It was a scorching, merciless world. The only alternative to Zion was death.

Ignorance is a relative matter. Kate, only half Jake's age, was better educated. But Jake remembered the world before the Apocalypse. He remembered the millions of people crowded together in vast cities. He remembered a bus ride across Nebraska, hundreds of miles planted continuously with grain. He remembered the many conflicting religions and the arguments, fistfights and shootouts caused by them.

And he knew things. True, many of the Saints and Mothers knew the same things. But the Mothers had convinced themselves that such knowledge, their very memories of the past, was false or irrelevant, possibly even sinful. The Saints were beyond disobedience, beaten down, dependent on the Mothers' leadership for survival under the harsh post-apocalyptic sun. Probably some of the other Saints were, like Jake, cagey: they knew Zion was a living lie, but one they had to go along with to survive. But Jake had never met one, that he could tell.

The Children he liked well enough, just as he liked the Mothers and Saints well enough. There was no hatred even for the Mothers simmering beneath Jake's surface composure. He knew that the Mothers were full of shit in a lot of ways, but he also knew they had survived when every other group had failed.

But Kate was in a category by herself. Alone among the Children, as far as he could tell, she wanted to know what was going on. The problem presented was two-fold: she was unlikely to believe him, and if she did what would she gain from it? If the Mothers lied about the past, and Mother Mary, that did not prevent them from having a stranglehold on the present.

"Working late again," he said.

"I like it," she replied.

"Have you found anything interesting?" Jake ventured.

"Maybe. But how can you know, if two people tell you different things, which one is true? I mean if you cannot just check for yourself, like something that happened in the past."

"There was a saying before the Apocalypse: 'Those who do not know the past are doomed to repeat it.' But the Mothers teach you about the past. And now you teach the Children in their turn."

"You lived before the Apocalypse, right?"

"Yes, I was born in 1979."

"And is what the Mothers say true?"

Jake had known this question was coming, but he had not known what he would say. "They say you were born before the Apocalypse. Is that true?"

"I do not know," Kate admitted. "Where else did my genetic material come from?"

"You are the scientist, I am just an ordinary Joe who did not die when almost everyone else did. I did not meet you before the Apocalypse, but there were lots of people back then. Not like now."

"How many people?"

"They say there were about 250 million people in the USA, and about, I do not know, five or six billion people in the world."

Kate had seen the figures in the Magic Encyclopedia, but had never been able to believe them. Her head started doing automatic calculations: they were resurrecting about a thousand Children a year, so it would take a thousand years to resurrect a million Children, and a thousand thousand years, a million years, to resurrect a billion.

"And Mother Mary and Jesus killed them all," she said, wanting to cry.

"I would not say that," offered Jake. "To tell the truth, I never saw Mother Mary or Jesus either. They all died of disease and war and famine. It was too many people, I guess. Just too many people. Swimming in their own piss."

"Swimming in their own piss?" Kate was confused.

"Swimming is how you get through water. Piss is urine. Six billion people pissing everyday, eating, breathing, getting in each other's way."

Kate's head started calculating again: a liter of piss per person, six billion liters a day, sure you could swim in it.

Suddenly Jake felt panicky. "Look, Kate, do not tell anyone any of this. I am not sure what the Mothers will do to you, but they would kill me."

"Kill? Certainly they would not do that."

"Certainly they would. Be careful. Do not get caught. I will be around." And he fled the room. Thinking how stupid he had been.

He had to escape. Even if he would be forced to live alone like a hermit. He had seen the weeds beginning to grow again. If he got away from Zion, he might survive. He would need water, extra clothes, and most of all food. A good knife, somewhere there had to be a knife he could grab. Maybe he could even steal a car. But probably it would be too big of a chance, he had not ever worked in the garages, they might be guarded.

Chapter 13

It being a typical day, he dreamed of killing Saint Sarah Jefferson. Instead he cut a head of cabbage from its stalk and placed it in the box with the others, completing the box. His back ached as he stood. Then he quickly squatted back down to pick up the box, trying to keep his back straight as he lifted it. He moved quickly across the field to the wagon, where another Saint received the box from him. Then he went back towards his row of cabbage. He hated harvesting cabbage. It was just as boring as any of the other work he did, but the cabbages were heavy, so the physical pain reached greater proportions.

He could, of course, kill Saint Sarah Jefferson with his knife. But his own end would come moments afterwards. Saint Paul Willscams had no desire to lose his life just to kill Sarah Jefferson. But if there were any real men among these Saints he worked with, if a mere twenty men would go with him, he might chance it. Surely most of the Saints hated the Mothers as much as he did. They would have to kill some of the Mothers and find where the guns were stashed. That was the only reason the Mothers could keep them subdued: guns versus knives.

His body working on automatic, Saint Paul was free to dream. There had been two rebellions of the Saints that he knew of, in addition to the two fights among the Mothers themselves. One came shortly after the Mothers asserted their full control of Zion in 2004. By then Zion was reasonably secure from outside attack; most people outside Zion were dead, or came there as pitiful refugees. Food was extremely scarce and work was extremely hard. What had been a division of labor was beginning to look like slavery, especially to the agricultural workers, who were mostly men. Many of those men, like Paul, had spent their lives giving orders, not taking them. Several thousand farm workers went on strike, asking for an elected government and the old basic rights of free speech, free association, and freedom of religion. If they had known how the Mothers were going to respond, they probably would have gone about the whole thing differently. The Mothers came in with rifles and made some speeches about it being an emergency situation that would improve eventually with the Grace of Mary, and ordered the Saints back to work. Someone yelled "Go to Hell," and someone, maybe the same person, was shot dead. Then they hauled away a group of ten men and shot them. A number of Saints used the occasion to escape into the wilderness, where they probably died within a few days. The rest went back to work. The worst part of that year, Paul remembered, was the intensification of religious instruction. That was the year talking while working became punishable by death. No talk, no revolt.

His life had started out so grand. Paul Willscams III was born in the beautiful city of Seattle in 1964. His father was a third generation lawyer; his grandfather was a founding partner of the city's most prestigious law firm. He grew up loved by his mother and father and cared for by a series of maids and au pair girls. At the age of fourteen he began paying them to have sex with him. Excelling at an exclusive private school, he envisioned a career in politics. His friends were the sons and daughters of the city's most powerful men and women. Then, off to Harvard, followed by Yale Law School and immediate entry into the world's most powerful law firm, Rockefeller, Kennedy, Bush and Hoover in Manhattan. He was hard working and brilliant, bound to become a partner. Of course his family would have liked him to practice in Seattle, but they understood that New York City was where the real power was. He married a Yale graduate from a powerful family with old but still perfectly good money, Emily Cooper, and had a son, Jonathan.

Oh, the fights they had had defending such clients as General Motors and RJR Nabisco. Only a fool dared attack a company defended by Rockefeller, Kennedy, Bush and Hoover, especially if the young Willscams fellow was assigned to the case. In 1995 he became a partner. Life was great.

1998. That was when the world turned evil. Emily and Jonathan were among the first to die of the plague. One by one the employees of the firm went to the hospital, never to return, messengers and legal secretaries, associates and partners alike. When the Plague was over three-quarters of the firm were dead. Yet litigation went on. He persevered. Discussed becoming a senior partner.

But the following year Manhattan, briefly quiet and seemingly deserted, became a war zone. Bankruptcies put an end to litigations that the Plague had been unable to stop. Paul assessed the situation, the real threat of being caught in Manhattan as society collapsed, and returned to Seattle, to an opening at Riddles, Willscams, Bullets and Talkingshams.

Even then he had hope. He had an affair with one of the secretaries, thought of marrying her and starting a family again. She introduced him to the Church of Isis, which managed to remain life-affirming despite the disasters that had engulfed the world. He began sleeping with other women he met at the church, and came to the attention of the Church hierarchy. They began to take some of their business to his firm. The economy even picked up a bit in late 1999.

But the world continued to fall apart. Weather became even more erratic than it had been in the 1990's, and the thinning of the ozone layer began to affect plant life. Food became expensive, though there was plenty if you had the money. Most people in the Church of Isis volunteered at farms they had established, and Paul did too. It was not bad, working in the fields for a day and having an orgy at night.

The government did not collapse, it withered away. It tried delegating authority to the States, but essentially found itself in an unwinnable war with the Army of God, which had gained thorough control of the Bible Belt. Paul became part of the Army of Isis, as did everyone else in the Church. When the Army of God came to Seattle in the spring of 2003 the people of Seattle put up a stiff defense. After two weeks of fighting it became apparent they would have to retreat or die. There was only one choice remaining for the worshippers of a female Deity: Zion. Only that region had the strength to resist the Army of God. And in 2003 the Church of Mary was still practicing a degree of tolerance, at least for the Church of Isis and the Church of Mary Immaculate.

His father, Paul Jr., advised Paul to stay in Seattle and join the Army of God's Kingdom of God. "Look at history, son. Fighting just isn't worth it. We're lawyers. Commerce will start again once the Army of God has clear authority. People will need lawyers again. Chances are you'll get killed on the way to Zion. You know that an army of women is no match for an army of men. And if you don't get killed on the way to Zion, sooner or later the Army of God will overrun Zion. They may not accept surrenders so easily there."

But Melissa, Erica, Joan and Patty had more powerful arguments to make. To their surprise, the Army did not chase them as they retreated towards Canada, preferring instead to consolidate in Seattle. Avoiding Vancouver, their column of some 15,000 people met only the most minor harassment in its flight east along Canada's Route 1. They were greeted warmly when they reached Zion. When the men were separated from the women to do agricultural duty they did not complain; everyone agreed on the importance of food production.

To everyone's surprise the Army of God simply collapsed the following year when the crops in the territories they controlled failed. That's when Paul tried to speak to the Mother who was their overseer. He remembered the conversation clearly.

"Now that it's safe, I'd like to look up my old friends, the people from the Church of Isis I came here with."

"The Church of Isis no longer exists. We've been saved by the grace of our God, Mary the Mother of God. Your job is to honor Mary by growing food for all her children. As a man that is what you are fit for. Haven't you been listening during the evening prayer services?"

Once he had defended a pesticide company against a lawsuit filed by the United Farm Workers. Now he was being told what to think by a woman who for all he knew hadn't completed high school.

A sharp pain brought him back to his senses. He had cut himself with his knife. What folly, he thought. How long can this go on? He finished filling his box, then took it to the cart. He did not mention the cut, but the dripping blood was obvious. "You had better go clean that wound off and bandage it," said Saint Sarah, "but don't be slow about it."

Chapter 14

"Mostly we learn by doing. The theoretical background from your studies will help you make sense of this, but there is no substitute for actual practice." Kate used the same didactic speech pattern that she had learned from her teachers.

Ann just nodded her head.

"Chromosome analysis and reconstruction is the most critical step of the entire process. If it is not done correctly, then the whole project will fail. Sometimes the process fails at another point, for instance when the nuclear material is inserted into an egg or when the fetus implants with the growth chamber. But in that case we can keep putting the good nuclei into eggs until one takes properly. On the other hand if a nucleus does not take on repeated tries, that is an indicator that we failed to properly construct it."

"Where do the ova come from?" asked Ann.

"The ova are created in ovarian cultures. That is a very complicated process in itself, and very important. Once a healthy ova is produced the nucleus is removed. In fact the nuclei from these ova are the main source for the DNA used to reconstruct individual's genetic codes. All humans have very similar genetic codes; that is what causes us to have human bodies instead of animal ones. At most about one-half of one-percent of the code varies; that small bit is responsible for our physical individuality. In the process of resurrecting an individual that small subset of the DNA is spliced out of a complete set of genes that is derived from the nuclei of the ova. The individual parts are created in a gene sequencer based on the computer record of our analysis from the former body of the individual. Most of them are very standard; we just find out which standard sequences a person has, and then plug them in. Conceptually simple, but in fact a complicated and tricky thing to do."

"So," said Ann, "if you want to, you can make a person identical to their prior life, except maybe to change the color of their eyes or hair, or something."

"I suppose we could. But we do not. Each Child has a gene code identical to the former body. I suppose that makes it easier for the soul of the former person to reinhabit the body."

"I see. How do you think the soul was matched up to the body, the pre-resurrection body, in the first place?"

Kate felt her pulse quicken. "You could ask one of the Mothers. Maybe they know."

"If you do not know that, how can you know about the soul when we were dead?"

"The Mothers know that kind of thing. Our job is to create the bodies to hold the souls. Maybe our souls were shaped by our bodies during our earlier lives. They would not have had any memories before we were born the first time."

"They start teaching us memories when we are very young," said Ann, challenging Kate. "We remember what they teach us. Sometimes I think I cannot remember my past life at all. Maybe they tried to teach me the wrong one."

"Listen, Ann, maybe you cannot help but think such thoughts, but you had better be careful about stating them. I have heard stories ... well, the Mothers do not like anyone doubting them. They could give you a menial job, a really hard job on the farms. Or they could kill you. If you want to ask questions about how we do the resurrection, fine. But do not start questioning our theology. You are the same Ann Swanson who died before the Apocalypse. And you have to learn how to resurrect other people. Call it science or call it a miracle, it is what you have to do."

"Maybe I do not care what they do to me. I was dead once, I can be dead again."

"Look, Ann, I have the same questions. You are not alone. But you have to be careful who you talk to. We will talk about this more. But let me show you this computer program now. Please?"

"Yes, there does not seem to be a reason to talk about souls. I am here to make bodies, and the Mothers will give them memories, and they will grow food and some of them will make more bodies still."

"As you doubtless know from your lessons," Kate lectured firmly, "computers are used to process the information created in the complex task of analyzing and recreating the genetic code..." And the lecture went on, with Kate showing Ann some of the actual tasks where a human monitored or intervened in the process.

Ann liked Kate, but as the weeks passed she had increasing difficulty acting appropriately with the Mothers and her fellow Children. Her life seemed devoid of meaning. She began doubting first one thing, then another. She had begun by doubting that she was the same Ann Swanson as the woman who had lived before the Apocalypse. Then, since the Mothers had trained her to believe something that was not true, she doubted what they had taught her about history and religion. Perhaps people had been happy before the Apocalypse. Perhaps the good people had gone to heaven with Mother Mary during the Apocalypse, leaving the Mothers behind as punishment. Jake had indicated that life was better before the Apocalypse, and that he himself survived it while many better people died. Perhaps Mother Mary was not God. Maybe the false old religions were right, maybe God was male, Satan. But that was hard to imagine: why would God be a man? Maybe the Resurrection of the Dead was an entirely mechanical process, as was the birth of consciousness in a body; perhaps the prayers to Mary were superfluous.

Ann began to wonder if other people, besides Kate and Jake, had doubts. But she heeded the warnings of Kate and Jake and kept silent. After all, no one volunteered this information to her. She tried to think of ways she could ask the Mothers questions so as to judge their answers without getting herself in trouble.

"Mother Elizabeth Ann, can you tell me why Children are not able to remember the past without remembrance lessons?"

"Why, of course, dear. You should know that! Death was a real and at the same time traumatic experience. So the memories are buried. They have to be dug up. It is hard work, but you could do it by yourself. The Mothers just help the Children off to a good start. And now Children are starting to help Children. It is just wonderful. I almost wish I had been resurrected myself!"

As far as she could tell, Mother Elizabeth Ann was totally sincere and honest. She was always full of enthusiasm, even about the daily chores of the resurrection. In contrast Mother James Marie was much sterner. But Ann could not help but question her: "In the computerized reconstruction of an individual's genotype, I know that sometimes the misplacement of just a few DNA units, if they are crucial ones, can result in a failed resurrection. Does something similar happen during Remembrance if the Mothers try to teach a Child incorrect memories?"

"My, you are such a clever Child," said Mother James Marie. "I can see why they brought you here at such an early age. I suppose you are right. Things could go wrong with Remembrance. And then we might have to start all over again, would not we? But I could not tell you of a case of that ever happening, yet. I guess we are lucky the Remembrance process is more fault-tolerant than DNA reconstruction."

Ann did not know it, but that one conversation with Mother James Marie caused her to be brought under surveillance. It was not the kind of super-sophisticated, full-time surveillance of the pre-Apocalypse police agencies, but it was effective enough in the limited sphere in which Ann dwelt. Mothers who might ordinarily be too busy to notice how Ann reacted to a simple "Good morning" now saw that she was at best reserved and at times hostile. At public meetings it was easy to see a disdain for prayers and sermons.

The Mothers had dealt with discontent before: not only were Saints, who remembered the easy luxury and verdure of pre-apocalyptic times, prone to it, but occasionally Children and even some Mothers themselves developed problems. Usually they were able to isolate the disgruntled so that the contagion did not spread. Often the persons involved responded to prayer and therapy; sometimes they were reassigned to the most menial jobs; but there had been occasion to banish some to the outside world, where death was sure and swift.

Finally Mother Barbara sent for Ann. Much effort had been invested in Ann's education, yet it was clear that Ann resented her coworkers and superiors. Mother Barbara's job was to get the problem out in the open. Then, it could be corrected. Or eliminated.

Ann was almost relieved when she was called to Mother Barbara's office; she suspected it was because of her loss of faith. She was not afraid of the Mothers, despite the warnings of Kate, Jake and others. As a Child she had treated the Mothers with awe; they were the infallible goddesses who were a step away from Mary the Mother of God. Now they were bossy frauds; but she had not learned to fear them. She had seen them scold and inflict minor punishments on Children when growing up, but having been a model child had escaped even the light slap on the face or extra work details that had been all they needed to keep the children in line. Jake's hints were meaningless to her; despite their close physical proximity, the mental world of a Saint, survivor of the Apocalypse and slave to the Mothers, was unthinkable to the Children.

Mother Barbara did not bother to smile, or to ask Ann to sit.

"Ann Swanson."

"Yes, Mother."

"Recite the Mother's Creed for me."

Ann hesitated. She considered saying no. She began to realize she had gotten into something which fell outside her power. She began:

> "I believe in God, the Almighty Mother,
> Creator of all things visible and invisible.
> And in Jesus Christ Her Son,
> Born of the Virgin Mary,
> Her manifestation on earth,
> Who suffered under Pontius Pilot, was crucified,
> And by Her grace rose from Death.
> I believe in Their Church and Their Triumph
> Over Evil and Satan."

"And how much of that do you believe?" Mother Barbara asked when Ann was done.

Chapter 15

Jake did not try to kid himself about his political astuteness. He had done his best to survive, but he knew he owed a great deal to luck. If he had attached himself to the wrong sect at the wrong point, or even been in the right sect in the wrong city, he would have died. True, fools died inevitably in the Apocalypse, but people wise and strong were struck down just the same. In a world of 5 Billion people less than fifty thousand survived. The Mothers were wise, strong and lucky. He was a mere appendage to them.

Jake had often wondered whether the Zionists were truly the only group of humans left. Perhaps somewhere a man or woman, a family or a tribe had survived. But this was one topic of which the Mothers had spoken among themselves so much that the Saints could not but hear about it. Radio contact was lost with the few distant outposts of civilization one by one. During this time Zion itself went through years of crisis: hard work, hunger, and death. They solved the food problem even as they wondered why the women had stopped conceiving children. Even when the Resurrection process became reliable enough to compensate for the death rate, it produced Children who required years of care before they could contribute to the work needed for survival.

If there were other outposts, they were not communicating with Zion. Jake no longer believed there were other survivors. If they had the technology to resurrect people, or to deal with the sterility problem, they would be able to communicate by radio.

Still, he longed for freedom. There was no way to have freedom within Zion; even the Mothers were trapped in their own system. Yet to escape meant total solitude; he wondered if that would be any better. Plus, there was food in Zion. While there were signs that wild plants were beginning to return, that hardly meant he would be able to find enough to eat. Still, he had a stash of seeds to take with him if he did leave; if he could survive and make one harvest, then perhaps solitude would become his main problem.

He looked forward, every evening, to seeing Kate. Sometimes she was not in the computer room. Most of the time they just exchanged greetings. On the Third of April, 2028, Jake was pensive. He did not believe he had the courage to escape from Zion, yet he wondered if anyone lived outside in the wilderness. He wondered why he was so lacking in sexual interest, which itself was unusual. He was so accustomed to not being horny that it seldom occurred to him to even think about it. Kate and the other Children, male and female, he knew were not developing normally. The girls had no breasts, the boys no beards. You could tell that despite their loose robes. Was this a miracle from Mother Mary, a result of some post-apocalyptic environmental factor, or genetic manipulation by the Mothers? He decided he would ask Kate if she were there. She would probably know, and she could be trusted, as much as anyone could be trusted.

She was not sitting at her computer terminal. Kate stood staring out of the far doorway into the adjoining lab. She was quietly crying.

"Kate, what's the matter?"

She looked at him, closed the door to the lab, and walked towards her work space.

"Ann's in trouble," she said in a whisper.

"Could not keep her mouth shut, right?"

Kate nodded.

"There is nothing we can do," Jake counseled. "Maybe later. Look, they will be careful with her, gentle, she's valuable. We Saints are expendable, and maybe someday Children will be, but not yet. Maybe we will lose her, she will become a Mother herself, but I doubt it. She just has to learn to keep quiet. And that is what her punishment, whatever it is, will amount to. Teaching her to be quiet. To pretend to believe."

"Is this what life is?" cried Kate. "Lies and the creation and education of liars? I wish I had never been resurrected. I wish I could take Ann and go to the cities the Magic Encyclopedia describes. I wish I could change Zion. Why cannot they tell the truth? What would it hurt?"

"You did not live through the Apocalypse, Kate. They did. I did. It was horrible. Things are not so bad now. They might gradually get better. What you call lies are what once was called a faith. It allowed the Mothers to survive. You may not need it, but they do. Remember, they are getting old. They are already training you Children to take over. Then things can change. But in the meantime you and me and Ann have to hold our tongues. Just go along with things. I doubt we could survive outside of Zion."

"Outside of Zion," Kate whispered. She was lost in thought a long time before she continued: "We could live outside of Zion if we had solarfilm to grow food plants under. I had never thought of that. I can hardly conceive of being outside Zion. I kept thinking, dreaming, of going to the past. The past I already lived through, if you believe that. But could we leave Zion, you and me and Ann?"

"I do not think there is any way to escape carrying enough solarfilm with us to be able to grow enough food. But I have noticed something I wanted to ask you about. I have seen some plants growing wild. Here and there. Since about three years ago, and there seem to be more every year. So I figure the ozone layer is patching up, either that or some plants finally have become immune to the ultraviolet. Can you find out about that? Someone in Zion must be monitoring the ultraviolet levels. I will bet they already know when the corn and beans will grow unprotected again."

Kate's face had visibly brightened. "I can find out. I do not have any contacts with the botanists, but someone must be following that."

"Be careful," warned Jake. "That could be a dangerous question to ask."

"You are the one who should be careful Jake. Like you said, you are expendable, I am not. Look, we have already been talking too long. But let us continue to plan to leave Zion. I am beginning to hate it here."

"Sure. But from now on lets try to talk more indirectly about it. You do not have much experience with that, so just try to avoid talking about escaping. There is no point to risking being overheard."

"Okay. Bye, Jake."

"I will see you soon, Kate."

Kate had earlier informed Jake that, as far as she knew, Zion was rapidly escalating the Resurrection process. He knew that five years earlier only about three thousand successful resurrections were done each year. Already that had grown to over five thousand a year, assuming that she and her compatriots were successfully reconstructing a minimum of two genetic codes a day apiece. Six women, Kate and five Mothers, worked almost exclusively on computerized genetic reconstruction. But dozens of Children were in training in the Resurrection complex, and at least two would be assigned to her section when their training was complete. That would mean perhaps six or seven thousand resurrections a year. So in ten years, about, the population of Zion would double.

Work crews would have to build more greenhouses, and more crops would have to be planted and harvested. But there were not enough Saints left to do that much work. They were overworked as it was. So either more children would be assigned to menial labor, or they were going to begin growing crops outside the greenhouses, Jake figured.

Jake pondered these things as he completed his work. He recalled he had meant to ask Kate about the sex thing. That was not important, though, compared to having a partner to escape with. Then he would not be so lonely.

He recalled a man he had hung out with for a couple of years just before the Apocalypse, Tim McCleary. They had met in a jail cell in Dayton towards the end of the plague, and for no clear reason took to talking. Released, they decided to check into the Christian Vanguard Mission, which they had both been in before and thought was the best Mission in Dayton, overall. They ended up working in the kitchen together. They were both cynical about God and Jesus and Mary, but were careful to keep that from the others. It was dangerous to leave the mission, but they often did so they could talk without catching flak from the others. Tim had more of an education than Jake, having actually completed a semester of college. He would tell Jake about Philosophy 101 and science type things. Jake in turn told about his trip to California and the weird people he had met. Tim was funny; he could always twist something the Christian Vanguard minister said into its total opposite. But when Dayton was evacuated Tim was sent to Washington's Court House. The mission there was massacred by the Southern Baptist Army. Jake had never really had a partner since then. Survival demanded silence, or braying some prayer, which did not make much for real friendships.

Several weeks passed without incident. Jake saw Kate on occasion, but they did not risk a long conversation. Then Jake received another summons, this time to see Mother Gloria Anne. He had never met her, but he knew she was on the Council. Which meant no good for him: why would a Saint be called in front of a Council member, except to be questioned about his own conduct or that of another? It must be Kate or Ann, he thought. Yet Gloria Anne had merely requested his presence. And she was head of the technical services at the Temple of Resurrection. If he were to be interrogated about Ann or Kate she would have sent other Mothers to escort him. In effect, to arrest him.

With great trepidation Jake followed the instructions to find Mother Gloria's cell. When he found it another Mother was sitting at a desk in an outer room that led to the inner cell. She counselled him to wait. Perhaps fifteen minutes passed before two Mothers emerged from her cell, both women he recognized, scientists of the temple. As they left they ordered him to go in.

Two women sat in the cell. One sat in a chair with a sword across her lap. She looked at least 50 years old by the lines of her face; Jake had no doubt that she was handy with the sword. The other woman, who he knew must be Mother Gloria Ann, sat behind a desk, reading something. She finished and looked up.

"Saint Jake Thompson," was all she said.

"At your service, Mother," he replied.

"We all serve Mary the Mother of God," she corrected. "You have done well in her service. From most inauspicious beginnings, too. Years of agricultural service with no marks against your record. Almost two years now in the temple. I think that perhaps you are ready for more responsibility."

"If that pleases the Mothers," he said.

"You are younger than most of the Mothers, and most of the Children are far too young to accept major responsibilities yet. Yet responsibilities grow. Do you remember before the Apocalypse?"

"It was very bad before the Apocalypse," he intoned, automatically.

"In terms of sin, yes. But survival after the Apocalypse was very hard. Many people were worked to death, Mothers and Saints alike. Do you see what I am saying? For these few minutes at least, the two of us must talk about reality, not faith."

"Yes, Mother."

"A lot of pre-Apocalypse skills were lost with the loss of life. We have computer data bases that can be read to learn some of these skills. One of the skills that was partially lost was euphemistically called defense, which really meant war. You were never in the military, were you?"

"No. I did help defend the Mothers before and during the Apocalypse."

"Yes. Now, listen carefully. It is the wish of Mary the Mother of God that we train some of our people in the art of war. Mother Angela will be in charge. Her staff will consist of ten people. Four are Mothers, three are Saints including yourself, and three are Children. You will equip yourselves with the arts of war, and then train some of the older children, a hundred at a time, until you have about a thousand capable soldiers."

She appraised him in the silence. "Tell me what you think."

"I was hoping that ... there would be no more war. At least."

"I am still hoping that. It would not be held against you if you refused. You could still keep your position at the temple."

"I am sure I would not be asked unless it was important."

"Were important."

"Were important. What are we to fight with? What is the nature of the enemy?"

"Mother Angela will speak to you about that in detail. The truth, however, is that we are not sure. You are to train yourselves and your soldiers for the worst possibilities."

"Yes, Mother."

"I am satisfied with you. Do your best for Mother Angela. She will want to see you tomorrow."

"Yes, Mother Gloria Ann."

"That is all. Thank you for the work in the Temple. You may go now."

Chapter 16

"To be cast out is to die. In Mary Mother of God and Zion there is life. Outside of Zion lies Death. If you will not be a useful thread in the cloth of society, then you must be cast out. But there is still time to repent. Repent sincerely and you will be accepted into Zion and into Mother Mary's heart."

The four Mothers stood facing her. Ann was resolved to stand up to them. "Then cast me out," she said, unafraid.

So one of the mothers opened the door, and Ann walked from the dimness of Zion into the brightness of exile. The door slammed shut behind her, and she heard the motion of the bolt and crossbar being set inside.

For a minute she could see nothing.

In front of her the land was almost flat, with only the slightest change of colors to the grey-brown, barren soil. Scattered about were white shapes of varying sizes and shapes. These stretched towards the horizon, but were concentrated near the door and became less frequent in correspondence with the distance from it. She looked at a set of the white things that was close at hand. At first they were a confusing jumble. Then a textbook illustration matched itself, in her mind, to some of the objects: they were bones. Human bones. Skeletons.

The door was clearly visible in the box that marked the end of Zion. The box was grey cement and otherwise featureless. Ann realized it marked the termination of a long underground corridor. On the opposite side of the door the land was flat for a distance and then merged into low, well-rounded hills. Ann completed her walk around the building, carefully stepping over the bones. There was nothing else to note. She knew that Zion's above-ground farms were not too far off; she had walked to this point, she could walk back to Zion. If she could guess the proper direction. Even then, every door would be barred to her.

Overhead the sun sat at an angle in a deep blue sky. She felt a bit cool even with the sun hitting her. She had no plan. Walking, she found herself heading towards the nearest hill, hardly more than a mound; its mere existence was all that gave her direction purpose.

Hunger gnawed at her, but she ignored it, still focusing her mind on her confrontations with the Mothers. Ann had hardly noticed that she received no breakfast. In Zion calories were carefully measured; no one starved, but every man, woman and child was ready to eat when they sat to a meal. Hunger vanished with food in the stomach, but always returned well before the following meal. It was a cycle so consistent that no one gave it a thought. Yet it meant that Ann had little in the way of reserves to draw on.

The Mothers, a group of three of them, usually, had asked her questions, heard her argue, and sometimes argued back with her. The authority that each of them had should have been reinforced by their mutual support. Instead Ann's will seemed to grow stronger, as if it was a matter of life and death that they accept, if not her opinions, at least her feelings that she had a right to the truth.

"You say you do not think you are Ann Swanson?"

"Ann Swanson is my name. It is a name you gave me. It is the name of a dead person. I know all about her. But I am not the dead person. I have got her genes and her name. That does not make me her."

"You have her soul, Ann. Her soul and her memories. That means you are her. Your death was traumatic and you needed help remembering your past life. But you do remember it. You should not deny it."

"It is not a question of my denying it or not. It is not true. I was born here, in Zion. I was a baby here. I am not the resurrection of the adult Ann Swanson. In a way I am like her child, or a clone."

"Where did you learn the word clone?"

"It was in one of my courses."

"It was not used that way. It was used to indicate a cell splitting, and having two identical offspring. Where did you learn to call a human with identical genes a clone?"

"I do not know," she lied. She had learned from Kate. "It seems like a natural use of the word. I am genetically identical to the Ann Swanson who died in the Apocalypse."

"You are the Ann Swanson who died in the Apocalypse. You were resurrected by the Grace of God."

"I was resurrected by a bunch of technicians playing with DNA. You know that, so why do you insist God has something to do with it?"

"Because we know that God has something to do with it. God gave us the directions to follow to allow us to proceed with the resurrections. Where do you think the technology came from? Must Mother Mary appear to you every morning so you can eat breakfast?"

The argument had gone on and on, sometimes repeating itself exactly in wording, or with only minor variations. The only breaks had been for eating and sleeping.

She reached the top of the mound. Several skeletons kept her company. Were they from the Apocalypse, she wondered? But she correctly concluded that they were people like herself, people who had refused to obey the Mothers. Saints, mostly, judging from the hints that Jake had given her.

Then sun moved to her right and down while her hunger and chill increased. They, the Mothers, kill people. They must have caused the Apocalypse. They killed Ann Swanson and Mary Kate Ashton and the genetic predecessors of the Children. They killed all the other people too, and if Kate's hints were correct, they destroyed the lush garden that was the earth and all of its many people. They killed them for disagreeing or disobeying.

Ann prayed for Mary the Mother of God to crush the Mothers. Only then did she realize the absurdity of her thoughts. She had not really sorted through everything properly. What was God? The Mothers had taught her that Mary was the Creator of the Universe, which included Earth, the Sun, Moon, planets, and stars. She had crushed the evil men and those they had led astray in the Apocalypse, supposedly without the help of the Mothers. But if she wanted Zion, the perfect society, why had not she just created it in the first place? Why had she created evil men? Maybe the Mothers were lying about God. Maybe God had liked the men the Mothers called evil. Maybe God had nothing to do with it. But then how had it all come into existence? Ann's head swam.

At some point she realized she would die. Without food or water or warmth. Clouds appeared, thin clouds, but they filtered the sun and she began to shiver. If she were inside she would be warm, and could drink water, and could eat dinner. If she thought what the Mothers wanted her to think, or if she had taken the precaution of silence that Mary Kate and Jake advised.

She thought about the great river she saw on the way to Zion from Mother of the Holy Redeemer School. If she could walk to the river, or any river, she could at least have water. But she had no idea which direction to walk in. Nevertheless, she got up and walked down the hill towards where she had been cast out of Zion, towards the plain, figuring that was South.

At first the walking warmed her. She was cheered by the gradual diminishing of the number of human skeletons, and by the occasional sight of a wild plant. The plants were all of a kind: at most a few centimeters across, with dark green, skinny, waxy leaves radiating from a central core just at ground level. Ann could not know that these were the descendants of the common dandelion. Neither did it occur to her, despite her hunger, to attempt to eat the plants.

The sun disappeared behind clouds shortly before it would have touched the horizon. She felt she had made little progress, for there was almost nothing to mark it in the flat, dusty land. She could make out the low hills behind her, but not the outpost of Zion. Cold, whipped into her flimsy clothing by the wind, touched her soul. Tears salted her cheeks and death loomed before her mind. Fear overwhelmed her and her mind withdrew to a distance to watch her body cry as it turned back to Zion, running, hoping to find it before the sun dissolved into darkness.

Even propelled by terror Ann did not have the strength to run except at intervals. Her mind's eye pictured the familiar sights of Zion. She scolded herself as the Mothers had scolded her. Why indeed had she rejected the life that Mary Mother of God had conferred on her? Perhaps she was Ann Swanson, former nurse.

No, another fragment of her mind answered. She just should have kept quiet. She did not have to accept the lie. Their food and their housing was what she wanted. It was not that she minded the work. They had so much as said so: she had only to bow her head to their authority, and she could live.

The darkness and cold engulfed her. She thought she had seen the entry point, thought she had recognized the hills behind it, hoped she could keep on a straight course.

She almost ran into a skeleton. Even in the night the white bones were visible, and now they reassured her, telling her she was approaching Zion. The clouds broke above her, revealing stars, but she was too frantic to admire them. Instead she focussed her attention on the bone-yard, its ghostly white indicating the exodus point from Zion. She was near.

Ann pounded at the door, crying and yelling. She promised the Mothers her total obedience, but the door did not open. She kicked the door, but it did not yield. Death loomed; she realized the Mothers might let her die. Perhaps no one was even listening at the door; perhaps she would become bones to be pushed aside when the next trouble maker was cast out.

The cold numbed her arms and legs. She looked up at the stars, which were heaven, and her consciousness slipped away.

Chapter 17

Mother Gloria Anne prayed that Ann would repent and return to Resurrection City. Losing her daughter once had been bad enough. Losing her twice in one lifetime might be too much grief, even for one who had seen so much suffering. At the same time she was proud of Ann, who was willing to sacrifice her own life rather than deny the truth. Someday the Mothers would have to deal with the truth, or the Truth would deal with them. It was fine to have crafted a set of religious beliefs that allowed them to build a new society without the sickness of patriarchy. But they had substituted matriarchy, and Gloria had long ago concluded that the 'archy' was the real problem. Ann was no real danger to the Mothers. Telling the children where they really came from would not hurt them or the Mothers. But decisions had been made, and any who even discussed those decisions could be thrown outside even as Ann had been. Gloria remembered Samantha, dear Samantha, and how she had raged against the Catholic Pope. Gloria had been raised Lutheran, not Catholic, and of course the Lutherans had agreed to allow women to be ministers. But being a Lutheran minister was not what Gloria wanted anyway. Her husband,

Hubert, had been a Lutheran minister. Poor Hubert. Not a bad man, really, just conventional and boring, though that seemed oppressive enough at the time. Still, if she had known he was going to die in the plague in 1998 she would not have left him in 1995. He had been hurt, badly hurt.

Decades later, though, it still amused her to think of how he must have reacted to her joining the Church of Isis. He had tried to have a liberal attitude towards her mother, his mother-in-law, Liz, and her Church, but even though she was 2000 miles away in Los Angeles his true preference was to neither discuss nor think about the matter. From a distance the Church of Isis had sounded wonderful to her. It had the glamour of Hollywood, the mystery of ancient Egypt, the titillation of sex-worship, and the promise of miracles. Her mother occasionally appeared on the talk shows, dressed like a modern day Cleopatra, and admittedly looking more like 35 years old than her real age of over 60.

And the first few weeks in Los Angeles had been fun. Gloria had never slept with any man other than Hubert, but had thought about it a great deal. She quickly found herself three different boyfriends among the male church-gocrs, and even tried sleeping with some of the women as well. The training for the priestesshood that occupied much of her time was interesting enough. But her mother made up for lost years by paying too much attention to her. Mainly she wanted Gloria to be prettier, which involved losing weight, special exercises, and a variety of lotions and potions. Soon enough Gloria was looking much better, and being encouraged to sleep with local politicians and businessmen.

After six months she had had enough. To her the Church of Isis seemed as shallow as the Lutheran Church. She had gone back to Kentucky, wanting to be alone. It was just a few weeks later that she went to see a lecture, "The Female Nature of God." The lecturer, Samantha Franklin, impressed her as knowledgeable but not haughty. Gloria stayed for coffee afterwards. The circle of women talked for hours. Eventually Samantha had announced her visitation from the Virgin Mary. Her sincerity was evident, but Gloria took the story as a metaphor. Still, she joined the congregation the following Sunday, becoming its sixth member.

Then, truly, her life changed. The Virgin Mary did not visit Gloria, but Samantha was an inspiration. Her personal story came out in a humble, natural manner. Samantha had been raised Catholic and felt a special calling to serve the Virgin Mary. She also had studied some books produced by the women's movement and wanted to become a priest and reform the Church away from its patriarchal ways. She became a nun and pushed for reform within the Church, networking with thousands of like-minded American Catholics. But in 1994 the Pope declared that the possibility of women becoming priests was not to even be discussed by Catholics. Despite clear indications in the Bible that Jesus and the Apostles were themselves married and the fact that Catholic priests had been allowed to marry until the Middle Ages.

About then Samantha's parents died in an automobile accident, leaving her their house, an insurance policy, and an interest in a business her father had once owned. She left the Church and went to stay in the home in Winchester. Within a week she had been visited by the Virgin, who told her to start a new church. She was to teach that Mary was God, the creator of the universe, the Earth Mother, and the Eve who begat humankind. She was also the Virgin Mary who gave birth to Jesus, and it was her powers, not his own, that raised Jesus from the dead. Mary instructed Samantha to teach these simple facts and the doctrine that Mary had appeared to many people at many times in history, so that all the female gods were her manifestations. But there was to be no dogma, women had to search their own souls for their personal connection to Her. Even men could be admitted to the Church of Mary Immaculate if they accepted Mary as God.

Gloria helped recruit many new members to the Church. Some were women she still knew in the Lutheran Church in Lexington; a few were women in the Church of Isis. But most came from the Catholic parishes.

Looking back, Gloria knew that the recruitment was a matter of timing. In those final years leading up to the Plague and the Apocalypse many people switched religions and many new groups appeared. The Church of Mary and Jesus already had a huge following, but had started in Northern California and was just then spreading along the two coasts. The Church of Mary Immaculate had an open field for about two years in Kentucky and Ohio before they found themselves surrounded by the Church of Mary and Jesus. Then it was tough going, because scared people seek certainty, and the rival church was more than willing to give them certainty and orders to boot. They also sent diplomats to attempt to incorporate the Church of Mary Immaculate wholesale. But Samantha taught them they had more in common with the pagan, goddess-worshipping women than with the ostensibly similar authoritarian personality cult around Hilary Prophet.

When the Plague struck in 1998 they had forty thousand members, about four fifths of whom were women. The Plague threw everyone into grief and into survival mode. They were able to buy several large farms (you could buy almost anything for practically nothing at estate sales those last few years before money became a joke) and moved many of their suddenly unemployed members to the farms. Gloria's work continued to focus on bringing new people into the Church, but of necessity that meant finding them shelter and livelihood. In 1999, despite their own peaceful philosophy, they had to arm themselves against the civil disorders. Gloria had become a general, a role she never had imagined for herself. Everywhere you went there were dead people; only her faith in Mary sustained her in those years.

The year 2000 was a year of Panic, of scheduled elections, and of war. California and Idaho both attempted to secede from the union. A General Strike paralysed what little of the economy still operated, but was crushed by massive violence from employers and a government that still had troops at its disposal. Martial law was declared and elections were held, but if the new president had been installed, Gloria could not remember that. For her a more important event of the year was the Goddess Mutual Defense Pact, which included most of the female-based churches. They had to defend themselves against the several patriarchal churches having their own armies in the field by then, most notably the Army of God and the Southern Baptist Army.

Amidst all the tragedy, the worst for Gloria came in 2001, when Samantha was assassinated. They were never sure who was responsible, but they suspected the Church of Mary and Jesus more than the Baptists or the Army of God. Gloria took responsibility for the Church, and soon entered into negotiations to create the Church of Mary. She would have preferred to keep the Church of Mary

Immaculate separate, but the logistical pressure was too great. She hoped they would act as a sort of leaven within the Church of Mary, but the brutal reality of the eco-disaster was already following on the heel of the collapse of the old society. She knew young women who imagined that the collapse of the United States of America would bring a new dawn, an era of love and goddess worship among the forests of a restored nature. Instead the whole world was dying.

She was not even invited to be on the Council. But she was treated with respect, and helped develop the theology of the Mothers. The farms that grew the scant crops that kept them all alive came under her supervision. As an example to others she spent much time doing manual labor, planting and weeding and building the UV shelters. When the first power struggle came in 2005, she was one of the leading pragmatists. But things got worse instead of better. Even small points of disagreement became grounds for demotion or even exile, which meant death. A system of mind control was instituted, allegedly to protect the Children, but just as assuredly solidifying the power of the leading Mothers. Right down to forbidding people to use contractions as part of their speech. And, Gloria chided herself, she went along. Oh, she did what she could to keep inquiry and creativity from being totally stifled, but she convinced herself that the new system was necessary to survival, and that its success as a means of survival showed it was the will of Mother Mary.

They even admitted her to the Council of Mary in 2012 after Gray's Rebellion, an event that officially had not happened. And now she awaited word of her daughter, Ann, who was facing the horror of what lay outside Zion: a dead world.

Well, not quite dead. There are the Mexicans. And as fate would have it, I am supposed to find a way to help destroy them. But I'm sure that's not what Mother Mary wants. We are all her children. Perhaps I can find a way to sabotage our army. Perhaps there is still some way to bring freedom back to Zion.

Her telephone rang.

"She returned."

"Thank our Blessed Mother. And thank you for letting me know. Is she alright?"

"She is unconscious, probably from hypothermia or exhaustion. They are taking her to the clinic. She'll be fine, if her repentance was a true one."

I hope that she pretends that it is, thought her mother.

Chapter 18

Dreams plagued Ann's sleep. Skeletons danced about her, chanting bits of prayers. At times she wandered through hall after hall, sometimes trying doors, but all the doors were locked. An endless staircase became her treadmill, and she became colder and colder as she ascended, until she froze in place. She watched herself drawn piece by gruesome piece from a cauldron of body parts; a group of Mothers sewed her parts together and then threw her back into the cauldron, screaming.

She was hungry and needed to urinate. She was lying down. She wasn't cold and it was neither dark nor bright light. Am I outside, or inside, she thought, not daring to open her eyes. She noticed she was under a sheet. She might as well get it over with, she thought, and opened her eyes.

The room she was in was empty except for a bed, a toilet, and a table. One lightbulb lit the room; like almost all rooms in Zion, it was windowless. On the table sat a book, the Liturgy.

Ann relieved herself in the toilet and drank some water from the tap. Sitting back in bed, she wondered what was next. It occurred to her that if she had been cast out in the morning she may have been able to eat some weeds, get to a source of water, and even find a bit of shelter before night. She had seen lots of falling apart buildings on her car ride to Zion. How much cold did it take to kill a person? How much hunger? Did it matter? There was nothing outside, and inside there was only obedience.

She tried knocking on the door, but got no answer. Trying the door, she found it was locked.

I will be outwardly obedient, she told herself. I will pretend to be the resurrected Ann Swanson I once thought I was. I will do that for food and for warmth. Everyone else must know its a lie, all the Mothers and Saints anyway. They have all agreed to lie. They must have a reason for it. Probably to control all the Children. Maybe because if the Children knew the truth about the Apocalypse and what came before it, they would refuse to obey. The truth about what happened must be really bad. Probably the Mothers killed everyone who disagreed with them, and they had some weapon that turned the earth into a desert.

Hours passed and Ann alternated between awareness of her hunger and thinking. She thought about the history and theology she had been taught, and about science, and about her actual experiences in Zion. No definite conclusions came to mind, though occasionally connections were made that had previously eluded her.

Her daydream was interrupted by the opening of the door. Something hit the floor and then the door was closed again. On the floor was a tray with a bowl in it and a spoon. Closer examination revealed cracked wheat porridge. She did not care, she wolfed it down and filled her stomach. Not long after that she fell asleep.

When she woke it was dark. The lightbulb was controlled from outside, so there was nothing she could do about it. She moved carefully along the floor, hungry, hoping another plate of food would be by the door. There was. She tasted it, noted it was the same cracked wheat mush, and downed it. But now she was unable to sleep. She wondered what had happened to Mary Kate and to Jake. Were they in similar rooms somewhere? Or just doing their old jobs? Or lying outside, dead? She imagined being in the Temple, among the machines, with her pen making notes on clipboards. All those children, all to be engraved with memories of lives now buried outside in the desert. Why? To hide the reality. They had sprung from corpses. Unlike real children, who came from a mother and a father.

That must be the real problem, Ann concluded. There are no Fathers. There are male Saints like Jake and Ed and Jim, and male Children, but for some reason there are no Fathers. If it were the matter of a soul needing a body, it would be easy enough to put the soul in the body of a natural child. Unless the souls of the dead really were keyed to the genes they had possessed. But that was ridiculous. Everything was ridiculous. Fathers had caused the Apocalypse, according to the Mothers. Fathers had been followers of Satan. So maybe new babies would be followers of Satan. Maybe only those who had been true to Mother Mary before the Apocalypse could be trusted by the Mothers, who were not good. If they were good, why would they cast people outside Zion just for asking questions or wanting to know the truth?

On and on her mind wandered until she fell asleep.

The light came on, waking her. She looked, but there was no new food. They are going to kill me with boredom, she thought.

Eventually the door opened, but instead of a food tray three Mothers entered the room. She did not recognize any of them.

"Why are you not praying?" demanded one. "This is the time of prayer!"

"I am sorry, Mother. I did not know the time. I will pray now." Ann sat up, swinging her feet over the edge of the bed, and began the standard litany. The Mothers prayed along with her.

When they were done the smallest Mother demanded: "What is the sincerest prayer?"

"Work is the sincerest prayer," said Ann.

"Are you willing to pray sincerely?" said the same Mother.

"I obey the will of Mary Mother of God," said Ann.

"Come with us, then."

The small Mother marched ahead of her, the others behind. The hall was lined with doors like the one she had been imprisoned behind. At the end of the hall were bars, behind which sat another Mother, who stood to unlock the doorway for them to exit. Behind them the metal door slammed shut.

They walked her here and there, in a part of Zion she had never seen before. Finally she stood before a field that was sheltered by UV filters supported by wooden beams. There were no plants in the field. They turned her over to another Mother.

"The others will be here soon. They already know what to do, so I am going to show you. This is going to be a field of kale. These flats over here have kale plants that have sprouted. See how small they are? We are going to plant them about four inches apart. You take this stick and make a hole. You put the sprout in, then you pat the earth gently towards it like so. Now you do it. Right. That is good. You go right down this row to the end, it will probably take you the whole morning, then you will do another in the afternoon. It is good honest work. Be very careful when you bring an empty flat back and pick up a new flat. For Mary's sake do not step on any plants."

Ann had only done three quarters of a row when the lunch bell rang. She managed from time to time to look around and see who her fellow workers were. Most were male Children; she had never seen so many male Children at once. Some were female Children and a few were Saints, mostly male. She noticed that male Saints were much more different from female Saints, but that only subtle differences distinguished male and female Children.

She had counted fifteen days passing when she was summonsed to see Mother Barbara.

"Do you like working in the farms?" asked Mother Barbara.

"Yes, Mother."

"Would you prefer to work in the Temple?"

"Yes, Mother."

"Do you believe that the Children who are resurrected are the same people who died before or in the Apocalypse?"

"Yes, Mother."

"And who are you?"

"I am Ann Swanson. I was born in 1970 and died in the Plague of 1998. I was resurrected by the grace of Mary the Mother of God in 2013. I was a nurse before the Apocalypse."

"Very well. You are to report for agricultural work in the morning, but may return to your old dorm in the Temple and continue your instruction and work there after the lunch break. When you have proven yourself worthy of serving Our Lady Mary in the task of Resurrection, you will be taken off agricultural duty. You will tell no one at the Temple where you are working mornings; if anyone asks say you are reporting as Mother Barbara has instructed you. Is that clear?"

"Yes, Mother."

"My advice to you, dear, is to spend some time in prayer. Ask Mary the Mother of God to help you, to show you what is true."

"Yes, Mother."

"Now report back to agriculture. Tomorrow afternoon you can begin your work at the Temple. You have a lot of talent, Ann. Please don't waste it."

"Thank you, Mother."

Chapter 19

Ann was broken when she returned. Kate decided not to question her about her experience. Ann was no longer allowed to apprentice as a genetic reconstructionist, but still came several hours a week for instruction. Kate had to report on Ann weekly, and was told that Ann still might become a reconstructionist if she became trustworthy. But from Kate's professional point of view the new Ann was lacking in curiosity and liveliness. She was just going through the motions. Professionalism aside Kate was heartbroken at what had happened, and quite afraid that the same thing could be done to her.

Kate continued her forays into the Encyclopedia. She had arrived at the conclusion that even a systemic study of the past might not arrive at the truth. Too many people had too many reasons to lie, or to make honest errors. Yet she had formed a picture of the past, or at least the recent past, that seemed likely to be true. Human knowledge and technology had made considerable progress during the century before the Apocalypse, but the most important result had been over-population and the destruction of the environment. Three major religious groups, Buddhism, Christianity, and Islam, had contended with each other and with a basically agnostic rationalism centered around science, for the allegiance of the world's people. Probably there were about 6 billion of those people just before the plague that preceded the Apocalypse.

The Mothers and Zion owed their survival not to Mary Mother of God, but to several aspects of the Apocalypse. First, The United States of America was one of the least ecologically damaged areas of the world. Second, Christianity happened to be the dominant religion in the USA. Third, science was so developed in the USA that even most Christians had some understanding of it. Why the Mothers came to dominate among the survivors was unclear. The encyclopedias were all written before the Apocalypse; the Mothers did not figure in them at all.

Given all that, Kate had to go on with her life. Her life consisted of work, which had developed two segments: genetic reconstruction and helping teach the Children remembrance. She wondered at that combination. There were pressures to do ever more gene reconstructs; why then was she assigned partly to something that took considerably less skill? Kate guessed that she was being groomed to become a Mother, in the sense of being a supervisor. They wanted her to be aware of the entirety of Child development, from the removal of chromosomal material from corpses to the final training of the Children's minds.

In the eternal underground twilight of Zion the days passed without demarcation. The days of the week were not used, for the theological reason that they were meaningless against eternity, and for the practical reason that Sunday, the day of rest, had been abolished in the interest of survival. The calendar that was used was no longer dated from the birth of God, Jesus Christ, but from the Advent of Mary the Creator of All Things and the Mother of God. The calendar was useful in timing the development of embryos into Children, and for measuring the annual rate of progress of those children. The computer even flashed the date and time when Kate logged on, but each day was essentially the same, so the numbers were without meaning for her. Even the names of the months had been abolished; numbers sufficed.

It was 9/20/28 when Mother Elaine called her away from Remembrance class. She liked Mother Elaine, who was a happy woman known for treating people gently.

"You have been doing very well helping the Children with Remembrance, Kate. I have been told that you are very good with computers, and excellent in your primary duty, which is genetic reconstruction."

Kate warmed to the praise. "Thank you, Mother."

"We, the Guiding Mothers, including myself, want you to try working at a higher level of responsibility. Of course, there are few duties requiring more of a person than genetic reconstruction. But within my domain, which is concerned with teaching Remembrance and with educating Children in general, there is much more you could be doing.

"The education of Children is essential to Zion. While it is true that we are guided by God herself, many things can go wrong in the development of a child. Take, for instance, the problems that Ann Swanson has been through lately. Perhaps there is something we could have done in raising her that would have prevented her troubles."

"Yes, Mother."

"You work with Ann, do not you? How is she doing?"

Kate had worked out an answer long in advance. "She's good at genetic reconstruction and I would be happy to have her assigned there permanently. Her absence created extra work for the rest of us."

"Yes, I am sure it did," chatted Elaine. "Still, I think it will be a long time before she can be entrusted with any great responsibility, despite her talents. You are a very perceptive Child, I am surprised you did not notice that Ann had problems. Perhaps if we had worked on them earlier straightening her out would not have been so traumatic."

"I am sorry Mother, perhaps if I knew what was wrong with her or how she was straightened out, then I could think back and some element of her behavior would stand out as an indicator. But I cannot think of anything, except perhaps for her reluctance to leave the reconstruction area."

"You yourself spend a great deal of time in the reconstruction area, do not you, Kate?"

"Yes, Mother, there is always work to be done."

"That there is. Now, I need someone to do Remembrance reconstruction. You have worked with the files that we use to do Remembrance work with the Children. What you will do now is help to construct the files.

"I am not very familiar with genetic reconstruction, but there must be many similarities. A person's life is a complicated thing, and most records were destroyed in the Apocalypse. Just as you have a human genetic baseline, we have a Remembrance baseline. The purpose of the baseline is to fill in gaps in our files that are missing, and to assure the viability of the child development process. In some ways it is more complicated because we have to use many variations in the scheme. We can't be having everyone with the same past life. "

"Which brings us to an important subject: truth. Occasionally you will find something in a person's record that would have a bad effect on the child's development. Perhaps the parents of the person were not good people, by our standards. Perhaps even the person chosen for Resurrection by Mary Mother of God has a blemished past, one that might make you wonder why God would resurrect that girl or boy. It is important for you to think of death and resurrection as a sort of purification. By the grace of Mary the sins of everyone who survived the Apocalypse, and of every resurrected child, have been forgiven. Since we in Zion are without sin, and God wants us to stay that way, we do not re-introduce sin in any form into a child's life. By the standards of Zion these children's pasts are those of saints. Let me assure you, by the standards of the evil world that existed before the Apocalypse, all of us are indeed saints."

"If children think they are good, they will be good. And these children were good in their past lives. Maybe not perfect, maybe not as good as they will be in this life, but good enough to be chosen by God for resurrection. That is the Truth, the real truth about them. So there is no need to tell them they were bad in the past. If they remember it on their own, fine, we will help them deal with it. Do you understand?"

"Yes, Mother," Kate replied. Then she took a calculated risk. "Has anyone ever?"

"Ever what, dear?"

"Have there been cases of Children remembering sins from before the Apocalypse, without being taught in remembrance?"

"Of course! But we do not encourage people dwelling on it. Now, you will be working with

Mother Mary Scott, and she is training two other Children right now. They are the first who have been assigned to this task. Of course you understand that this is a very sensitive job. Access to the records of the past is a great responsibility, and a great trial, because it exposes you to the old, bad world. But do not be afraid, all of the Mothers survived that world and the Apocalypse, and you only have to deal with its shadow. Let us see, oh, yes, the other girls names are Rebecca Highsmith and Georgina Washington. I am sure you will like them."

"I am sure I will, too."

"Good. Saint Ann will take you to Mother Scott. Go with the Grace of Mary."

"Thank you, Mother."

Mother Mary Scott was old even for a mother. Grey hair stood in sharp contrast to her deep chocolate-colored skin. Despite her age she was both energetic and busy. They were perpetually behind in their work, she explained; there simply were not enough people assigned to it to keep up. In fact they were all very busy at that very moment, and her time could not be taken up teaching Kate until things were more under control, but Rebecca could give her a tour and she could fetch things for them until they worked through the backlog.

As soon as they were out of earshot Rebecca whispered, "I have been here maybe half a year and I spend most of my time fetching. Georgina has been here longer, but she would be fetching too if Mother Elaine had not said something. Mother Scott looks over every file personally before it goes out. Everyone is too busy to teach you anything. I have compiled about a dozen files by working off-hours. But almost everyone here works almost every minute they are awake, so even in the off hours I am either looking for stuff or re-filing stuff. A lot of things are on the computer, I will show you that later, this room is church records. As you can see, the room is huge and there are a million files in it. A lot of files have not been sorted properly, we are so busy, and a lot of the files were in very bad shape when they were found. So things often are not in the order they are supposed to be in, alphabetical or chronological, usually. The churches are arranged geographically by town or county, that is their names before the Apocalypse, which you will have to learn. There is a big map over there, see it? And there are maps on the computer. There is Mother Sharon, she is from Selection, stay out of her way if you can."

"Selection?"

"Well, what do you think, Mother Mary stands over graves and points? This is not official, but as I figure it they find a graveyard and take samples. They get the names off the gravestones, which are markers that go with each grave. Some churches have their own graveyards, those are the easiest, but mostly each town has a graveyard so you have to figure out who went to which church. Anyway Selection looks at the DNA and the Church records and decides who gets resurrected. You would think they would just go ahead and do the remembrance files since they have most stuff sitting in front of them to make their decision. But no, they give us the name, date of death, and church, and we have to construct the whole life history. I guess Selection just wants to know what church you were in when you died; we have to dig a lot deeper to reconstruct someone's life. Now here is the file Penny Danjou for Lifeforce Baptist Church in Washington's Court House, Ohio, and back in go her church records, but she was only there three years before she died so follow me and we will enter the concordance room to re-file Penny's birth and death certificates."

It turned out that the areas devoted to records were even larger than the Temple of the Resurrection proper. In addition to the Selection department and Kate's Remembrance department, there was a group of Saints supervised by a Mother who did nothing except take in new documents and put selected information onto the computer system.

As Rebecca predicted, most of Kate's time was occupied filing or retrieving documents for the Mothers who prepared the files. Though Rebecca and Georgina also spent much time fetching, and the Mothers themselves often went chasing after information, the brunt of the work soon fell upon Kate. This did not bother her, however: she liked looking at the old records. They confirmed for her what Jake and the Encyclopedia had told her: while the Apocalypse might have been terrible, before the Apocalypse life had been much better for most people. You could walk outdoors, there was no shortage of food and much more variety, and there was a freedom, the ability to choose who you would associate with and what you would believe.

Kate was also given a pass code for the computer system. One of her first surprises was that the Remembrance group had unrestricted access to the Encyclopedia. She wondered if any of them had looked through it as she had, but she saw no signs of that and dared not ask. The phrase 'for the Children's sake' was repeated in Remembrance like a litany. Kate realized that most of the Mothers knew what life was like before the Apocalypse. For them, it did not matter: either they were afraid of each other, or they all felt that the creation of perfect Children required their playing along with the massive illusion that had been created.

After perhaps three months of attendance, averaging six hours a day at each of her two jobs, Kate found herself alone in the Remembrance work room. She had learned that the computer kept a record of all entries, and that sometimes a Mother would check over them to see that everyone was doing their work. But she had learned the entry code for one of the Mothers, and she figured Mother Scott was far to busy to more than glance at the logs. So she pulled up her own file and that of Ann Swanson, printed them out, and pinned them inside her gown.

Even trying to read her own file was dangerous. Like everyone else she bunked in a room with so many others that privacy was very unlikely. Her only chance was reading it late at night while doing genetic reconstruction.

Reading it, finally, was a disappointment. It covered everything she had been taught, and added nothing.

Several nights later, she handed Ann's to her, warning her that she had to read it and destroy it.

Chapter 20

Once there was a ship of fools. Sailing out into the ocean in winter, they complained of the cold, for they had not brought enough fuel for their fires. One wealthy cold fool said, "I'll give a dollar for each bit of fuel that is brought to this stove, to keep it going and keep me warm." Then one of the other fools, wanting to arrive rich at their destination, brought a chair to the stove and received a dollar, and they were warm for a while. Then the fool thought "This ship has much wood that we really do not need to sail across the ocean. Take this gunwale." And so he took a piece of the gunwale, and brought it to the stove, and received a dollar. The other fools saw this and they too started taking bits of wood from the ship, either to warm their own fires or to sell for money. One fool, who was not quite as foolish as the rest, worried, telling everyone that they would never reach land if they burned all the ship. The other fools said to him: "But we have taken many pieces of wood from the ship, and the ship still sails. The wood is more valuable burned than as part of the ship. You are such a fool! With our practice we will be warm, and rich, when we reach our destination." Then they threw the panicking fool in the brig for felony conspiracy to commit a misdemeanor. Slowly the ship began to disappear. Finally, one fool pulled up a plank from below the water level, and the water rushed in, and all the fools were drowned.

No one thing brought about the Apocalypse. Not the Catholic Church's stand against birth control. Not the Dupont corporation's twenty year campaign to continue manufacturing CFC's after it was shown they would deplete the ozone layer. Not the cutting of the Brazilian rainforest, not American's love affair with their automobiles, not the FBI's campaign to destroy Earth First! and the Industrial Workers of the World, not George Bush's desire to help his friends help themselves to the fruits of America's public lands. Nor the Norwegian's thirst for killing whales nor the Japanese and Taiwanese fishing fleets that scoured the Seven Seas of their fishes.

People think of plants as simple, but in fact they are far more complicated than any machine that humans have ever built. Some, it is true, are quite delicate, capable of surviving only in the most pampered of situations. But most have evolved to possess a great degree of flexibility. Has the average ultraviolet exposure increased by 10% because of the Dupont Effect (the depletion of the ozone layer by CFC's)? Most plants in fertile soil and a normal climate can cope with that, though they might not be as healthy as they would be under a normal sun. Is the soil depleted of nutrients? Many plants can deal with that as well. Has global warming caused slight changes in rainfall or extreme temperatures? Most plants have enough flexibility to deal with that.

But put all those factors together, too much ultraviolet, worn-out soil, and extreme temperatures, and a plant that might have survived one problem will most likely succumb to the combination.

The Apocalypse represented not just the deaths of individual organisms, but the collapse of ecosystems. Plants that might otherwise survive will not be able to reproduce if the bees, moths, and flies that cross-pollinate them have disappeared. Then again if the parasitical Ichneumonidae have been destroyed, those tough plants that can deal with drastic conditions may simply be overwhelmed by rapidly multiplying Lepidoptera larvae.

Perhaps the straw that finally broke the camel's back, the last major impetus that caused the collapse of Nature on every continent and in every ocean, was The Plague. This may seem surprising, since mankind has to take sole responsibility for the eco-collapse. The population explosion was said by many to be leading to global destruction. Shouldn't the reduction of the population by about 4/5ths have averted the eco-crisis?

Three major trends were too far gone to reverse, at least immediately, in 1998. Ozone destruction results from the slow drift of CFC's up to the stratosphere, so that the CFC's destroying the ozone layer in the year 2000 had, on the average, been manufactured between 1970 and 1980. While the use of petroleum and coal plummeted in 1998, the gasses that had entered the atmosphere since the beginning of the industrial revolution continued to trap sunlight with the greenhouse effect. And the breakup of eco-systems by urbanization, conversion of wilderness to farmland and grazing land, and the proliferation of roads, as well as more subtle changes such as the elimination of crucial biological vectors in a cascading effect, continued unabated.

But the surprise for the few people who could take time to think about anything but immediate survival, was the devastating impact of the sudden absence of man. Almost all of the earth's fertile land had been converted to farmland. Most of that farmland had become dependent on the use of chemical fertilizers and pesticides; much of it relied on irrigation. The soil had become practically sterile. Suddenly 4/5ths of the farmland was not needed to grow food, but this land did not start healing and returning to wilderness. The food crops that had grown on it were quickly destroyed by insect pests and molds. The weeds that tried to colonize the areas could not prosper in sterile, nutrient-poor soil, especially with erratic weather and the need to constantly repair the damage increased UV radiation was causing. By the year 2000 most of the farmland that had been abandoned had become semi-desert. The process fed on itself. Water continued to remove nutrients, and often the soil itself; wind whipped up dust-storms that smothered both the remaining farms and any plants that had somehow held on. Humans continued to die at a rapid clip, causing more farms to be abandoned. As chaos grew the human infrastructure collapsed. By 2001 it was practically impossible to buy pesticides or fertilizer or parts for broken equipment. Wandering bands of desperate people plundered farms that still functioned. Starvation became a major factor in the continued reduction of the human population. Whole regions baked because there was no vegetation to ameliorate the heat; the changed weather patterns caused a drop in rainfall, so that the deserts expanded their boundaries by hundreds of miles each year.

The Gobi Desert marched across China and Siberia. The Sahara sped southward, eating up the savannah and then the tropical jungles, and northward, leaping the Mediterranean to gobble up Europe. The Kalahari desert engulfed southern Africa and raced northward to meet the Sahara. All of the United States west of the Mississippi was desert by 2002, and spots of desert had appeared all over the eastern region. In the front lines of the deserts' marches were crowds of displaced locusts, rats, rabbits, humans and other animals that ate any living vegetation they could find. Even the Amazon basin, with its plentiful rainfall and vast areas of untamed wilderness, could not cope. There forest fires made possible by droughts gave the desert a foothold. The collapse in Brazil, though it had taken longer to start, was complete within three years.

Chapter 21

Ann Swanson, the angel of mercy, the nurse who cared for so many people during the plague, and who had died of it in 1998, was not just the child of two Lutheran Parents. She had been the daughter of Mother Gloria Anne, who now sat on the Council, who had left her husband and the Lutheran Church in 1995 to join the Church of Mary Immaculate, one of the predecessors of the Mothers.

Ann Swanson herself had left the Lutheran Church in her late teens and never joined any other church. True, she had been a nurse and died in 1998 during the plague, but the official cause of death was a drug overdose from pharmaceutical painkillers. She had committed suicide. So said the records Kate had smuggled to her.

I am not either of those Ann Swansons, she told herself over and over. I am not the Lutheran or the saint or the suicide. Before the Apocalypse everyone was born fresh, with no previous life. All the Mothers are doing is creating fresh people, babies, using some of the genetic material from corpses. I am more like Ann Swanson's sister. I have genetic materials from the same parents. What did Kate say? Some people were identical twins, two separate people with different personalities and souls who had identical genetic material. So I am the old Ann Swanson's identical twin. I did not become a nurse or commit suicide with painkillers. I was resurrected by the Mothers in the 13th year after the Apocalypse. I was educated by them. And some things they told me were true and some were false. And I have seen what lies outside of Zion, a dead world, and my only choice is to live with these Mothers. They want me to pretend I am the other Ann Swanson, so I will pretend, but I know I am not her. My only real memories are from this life, the other memories are false.

"Have you ever considered trying to change things?" whispered Ann to Kate as they both worked late at genetic reconstruction.

"You mean Zion? Sure, but I do not see how. I have had the idea to somehow try and tell all of the Children the truth, but the Mothers would prevent that easily enough and I would become one of those piles of bleaching bones you told me about. The other way would be to go along with the system and try to eventually make it to the Council with enough friends to make a change. That might work, but it would take decades. The Mothers almost never die, they have learned to stop most of the aging processes, so we could be stuck with them for eternity."

"Maybe," suggested Ann, "instead of trying to tell everyone we could just gradually gather people together, until we were strong enough to do something more."

"I talked to Jake about that," said Kate, "and he said it could be done on a very small scale, but sooner or later the Mothers will find out. He said there may even be more people who think like we do. Remember there are tens of thousands of people here, and we do not know very many of them. But you know how isolated the Mothers keep everyone. And any deviation from what they want invites questioning. No, I think our only hope is to escape. If only Jake were still working here we could probably form a plan."

"I would like to escape, but I have been outside. Twice. There is nothing to eat and it is cold at night. We could take some food with us, and some seeds to grow more food, but it takes a long time to grow food and how could we take an entire greenhouse? The food plants will not grow exposed to the raw sun. I do not see any plan that could work, not even with Jake."

"Then we will just have to wait. Jake and I think the sun is getting less bad. In a few years there might be plants growing wild. You said you saw some. Too bad you did not try to eat one."

"Sure, then if I lived we would know it was not poisonous. I do not know what will happen in a few years. I do not know how long I can pretend."

"Just keep trying. I am getting quite good at it."

Kate had managed to learn a great deal about the computer systems used in Resurrection City. Under the guidance of Mother Jennifer Civito, whose work team originally included several men who were later sent to work in the fields with the other Saints, it had been constructed from the best available pre-Apocalypse computers, using standardized software protocols (Tribble Objects), during the first few years after the Apocalypse. In the second decade after the Apocalypse a tremendous effort had been made to find and refurbish the machines that had made the computers. As a result all computers had become identical except for software. Each was a Silicon Graphics computer on a single chip. There was only one data storage device, the ReSearch Gigabyte module, and one printer, which was a dot-matrix printer modeled on the simplest machines of that type from the 1980's. In the rare case when more computer power was needed than was available on a single computer, it was borrowed from another one over the interconnecting network. Most computer users had only terminals, but because of the power needed for genetic reconstruction Kate's department not only had a fully working computer for each reconstructionist, it also housed a node of eight computers that acted somewhat like a supercomputer might have done before the Apocalypse. In fact, because the resurrection machinery also demanded so much computer power to control it, well over half the computer power in all of Zion resided in the Temple of the Resurrection.

Kate had learned the network protocols, so she could access any computer in all Zion. She had also learned SGC, the computer programming language at the core of all the computers. As a result she was confident that she could send a message to all the computer users, or to any subset of them, if she wanted. She had even figured out a way to do it without being discovered, she hoped: put the message in a remote computer and give it a time delay before flashing its message, then have it either erase itself or move itself to another location.

Kate considered trying the method she had worked out, but decided it was too dangerous. She could not be sure that whatever happened would not be traced to her in some way. When they escaped, she decided, she would have her program send out her message. In the meantime she used her knowledge of the system to learn as much as possible about Zion. That was how she learned about the War Department.

Chapter 22

Jake wondered if the creation of an army were a result of knowledge of a real enemy, or merely paranoia. Suppressing of internal rebellion was one explanation that he ruled out: it simply did not seem necessary.

As one of the ten centurions under Mother Angela, Jake had to work harder than ever before. They were told that their enemy was a group that had survived the Apocalypse and maintained the evil pre-apocalyptic ways. The enemy was far away, but was bound to attack Zion. The centurions were to train to defend Zion while provisions were made to attack the enemy.

To Jake weapons were the key issue, but Mother Angela was vague about what the enemy possessed. "Assume the worst," she had said, but then she had ruled out atomic weapons, major artillery and tanks. "For now our own weapons will be small arms and transportation will be by automobile and foot. If that is not sufficient I am sure our scientists can create heavier weapons."

Zion's weapons, he found, consisted of knives, a single model of automatic rifle, one type of high caliber machine-gun, standard mortars, and a few salvaged tanks. Training consisted of physical conditioning, hand to hand combat training, target practice, learning simple maneuvers and learning to follow orders.

The recruits were Children between the ages of 15 and 19. About one-third were boys. Jake was one of two male saints acting as centurion; both were pointedly given all-female centuries. Even so, in the other eight centuries the girls still were in a majority.

The original group of one hundred trainees became the non-commissioned officers of the little army. So Jake had ten young soldiers helping him train an additional 90 soldiers. These soldiers were told even less than the officers. "You have been selected by the grace of God to serve Her in a special way. Obey the words of your centurions and sub-centurions as if they were spoken to you by God herself."

There was no problem with disobedience. If Children were ever disobedient in Zion, Jake could see no evidence of it. Of course, the soldiers were specially chosen for obedience. They were not stupid, but they did not give the impression of being bright like Kate and Ann.

In addition to training the soldiers Jake had to make both oral and written reports to Mother Angela. He had trouble with writing, he was so out of practice, so one of his Children officers, Samantha, was promoted to be his secretarial aide.

The soldiers began to patrol the perimeter of Resurrection City. Possibly the Mothers had decided to sacrifice the outlying settlements, but Jake figured that they, too, had trained small armies. A number of outposts were established, allowing the sentries to view the outside terrain from the comfort of Zion. But patrols were also made on foot, as much for training as because they anticipated a real, immediate threat.

Larger training missions were also organized. The soldiers were issued special clothing and glasses to protect against the sun. Two in each group of ten were taught how to drive the automobiles that would transport them. They even drove some fifty miles, partly over rough terrain, and then deployed on foot to march ten miles to mount a mock attack. Jake was responsible for the supplies of his group, as well as for his soldiers, and was thus introduced to the problem of logistics.

With the help of the engineering team they learned to build simple bridges for the vehicles, and simple forts for defense. Jake did not know it, but the forts and bridges were little different than those used by Caesar's armies over two thousand years earlier.

Jake decided that he would commandeer one of the vehicles if they actually left Zion for an attack. He considered taking off from Resurrection City, but if discovered it would mean death. He might try driving in almost any direction and have a chance of avoiding all the Zionists, but given the certainty of eventually starting from outside Zion, he felt he could hold out for the better odds. In his imagination he pictured himself rescuing Kate and Ann from the Temple, Rambo style, but his rational mind, the survival mind that had kept him alive through the Apocalypse and Zion alike, ruled out that action as having no real chance of success. Unless, by some coincidence, he found himself near the temple with a rifle and an automobile filled with alcohol. He decided that he would take Samantha with him for companionship. If, after he had time to explain to her what had really been going on in Zion, she wanted to abandon him, he would not stop her.

Time passed and the army life became routine. About half the soldiers were assigned to a new agricultural substation; they worked hard every day and still had to keep up on their combat skills at night.

Over a year passed and Jake was beginning to like his new status as a Centurion when the usual staff meeting with Mother Angela was the occasion of the mobilization order. Mother Angela began by praising her Centurions' efforts, and assuring them of her confidence in their ability to wage war. She then told them that an expeditionary force would leave Zion in six weeks. A map of North America was unveiled showing Zion in white where Ohio and Indiana had once been. In what once had been central Mexico a much smaller area was marked out in red. Their objective was to defeat any defenses the enemy might have, restore them to the worship of Mary the Mother of God, and if necessary kill any person who resisted. She felt their army would be adequate for that if it arrived at their objective intact.

They would begin by heading west until they were on the western side of the Great Mother River, which Jake recognized as the Mississippi. Then they would head south along what had been Highway 35. She believed that course had the least number of obstacles to overcome; scouts had already travelled the entire route. Once in former Mexican territories they would take a route near the eastern coast until it was time to cut inland towards the enemy.

"The enemy speaks Spanish, which you and your soldiers will not be able to understand. Each century will be accompanied by a Mother who understand the language. They will not take part in the fighting, but will be in charge of converting the enemy."

Bad news, to Jake. What had they called such people, Commissars?

In addition to the thousand soldiers and twenty Mothers, there would be an engineering contingent and a "colony". "Ten engineers will come along with special equipment to help with getting across difficult terrain. The colonists will accompany us about half-way. There will be approximately 100 of them. They will be bringing equipment to grow food and produce other necessities. We have located a good site for them. Your soldiers will help them to get set up; basically we plan to build an entire small town in the space of five days."

Mother Angela went on about the expedition itself. Generally they would advance in a single file, with a regular marching order that just happened to put Jake's century in the center. The two fuel tankers would be about two thirds of the way back, with the colonists bringing up the rear. When they approached enemy territories they would break into two parallel columns and send out advance scouts.

Finally she asked whether there were any questions.

"Mother Angela, when will we be returning?"

"We will not be returning as a group. All of us will be staying in Mexico. Individuals may be brought back to Zion if that is the will of Mother Mary, but you should plan on staying there."

"What kind of defenses do the enemy have?" asked Jake.

"We do not believe they have any, but we cannot be sure. The key to victory will be surprise. If we can quickly infiltrate their cities then even if they have weapons better than ours they will not be able to use them."

During the remaining six weeks before departure they would have extra rations and intensify their drilling.

Jake began calculating exactly how he would escape on the way. He figured his best bet was to go south with the expedition but then cut east towards the Florida panhandle.

Chapter 23

Kate continued to explore the computer system. Together with Ann she put together a picture of the totality of Zion. They found that Resurrection City was more or less in the center of Zion geographically, so that escaping would not be easy. But they also found that Zion was thinly populated, with large deserted areas; by taking any of a number of routes they could leave Zion without coming within ten miles of a population. What they did not know was whether anyone would try to block their escape or come looking for them.

They decided to go east from Zion into former Pennsylvania on the belief that water would not then be a problem. Food would be a problem in any scenario they could imagine. Even if they carried seed corn or seeds of other edible plants, even if they were able to grow them under the unshielded sun, it would take several months between cultivation and harvest. Even allowing for survival on just one pound of food a day, they could not carry anywhere near that amount. They considered taking an automobile, but that had drawbacks: it would be difficult to get, and valuable enough to chase after. Even stealing the food would be dangerous: food was a valuable and carefully guarded commodity in Zion.

Despite the difficulties a plan started to coalesce. They would take one of the hand-trucks that were used to move equipment around the temple of the Resurrection. This would enable them to take about 100 pounds of supplies with relative ease. They would accumulate everything they needed except food in advance: seeds, simple tools, extra clothing, and cloth for a tent. Then they would grab the food in the middle of the night and make their escape.

Ann no longer had agricultural duty, but was still under surveillance; it was up to Kate to learn the art of theft. She began by learning to monitor activities in the city through her computer. A storage box in the Temple that was unlikely to be looked into was selected as a repository. Kate's first theft was from the Temple itself: a set of surgical instruments, valuable mainly for the knives. She emptied the set from the bottom of a stack of boxes; she was sure it would be months before the loss was noticed.

Obtaining seeds would be much more difficult. The agricultural areas, though huge, were far removed from the Temple, which would require her to avoid a number of human monitors. It was not clear exactly where the seeds were stored, either. What she thought she needed was an excuse to go in or near the warehouses she knew adjoined the greenhouses. She set out to learn more about agriculture from the magic Encyclopedia. One morning she awoke with the answer: she had only to go to the kitchens and take the whole grains or beans. Most likely they would sprout if placed in moist soil in spring.

She knew she could get to the kitchen areas easily enough, but food of all kinds was closely guarded or at least locked up. Her plan for the food was to break in the night they left; by the time the break-in was discovered the next morning, it would not matter. The seeds would have to be got at the same time.

She noted a new set of computer terminals that had gone on line, and upon checking it saw that Jake was one of the users. That let her know Jake's physical location. It seemed odd that a Saint would be allowed to use the computers, so she assumed that he used it only under supervision. It would be too risky to send him a message with it. Instead Kate and Ann altered their plan: they would pick up Jake on their way out of Resurrection City.

Finally the day had come. Kate planned to work late and put in a request that Ann be forced to assist her. Ann put up a bit of fuss, but was ordered by Mother Sarah Ruth to do the work. They worked as normal until 10:30 P.M. Then they uncovered their stashed goods and placed them on a hand truck.

Except for the newly formed army and locks on the food supplies, there was little reason for security in Zion, nor did many people stay up late. Still, Resurrection City was large enough to require them to walk for more than an hour to get to the soldiers' quarters.

They walked right up to a guard, a woman of about their own age.

"You cannot go in here," said the woman.

"We were requested to report to Saint Jake Thompson," said Kate.

"I am not supposed to let anyone in," said the woman, almost apologetically.

"Not usually, but look here are our orders, signed by Mother Tanya Jeane." Kate presented a computer printout with a flourish. The woman looked at it.

"I guess that is an order. I would show you his room, but I have to stay here."

"Thank you, Sister."

"You are welcome, Sister."

Jake was bunked in a room with three other people, and was sound asleep. It was difficult to wake him, but at last his eyes focussed on their faces. Ann put her hand over his mouth, then motioned him out of bed and out of the room.

By then Jake had sense enough to guide them out of the hall and into a storage room.

"Well, Children, I was not expecting to see you. In three days we are supposed to head to Mexico to conquer another group of people who survived the Apocalypse."

"We decided to escape," Kate said, "and figured you would come with us. The bags are full of supplies."

Jake sat down on a crate. "Yes, I was planning to escape somewhere along our route to Mexico. How many hours more until wake-up bells?"

Ann consulted a watch. "Only four. Kate said there would be a door near here to the outside. We were going to head east. There is more water in that direction, according to the Encyclopedia."

"We will not get very far on foot," said Jake. "We will have to steal one of the transport vehicles. They are already loaded with supplies and hopefully with fuel. Then let us head west. I have a good mind to warn the Mexicans about what the Mothers are planning."

"I do not know," said Kate. "The West was pretty dry even before the Apocalypse."

"Not that dry. We will not be going that far west. There will still be water in the Mississippi River. If things look bad we can always turn back east once we are well south of Zion."

"East, West, I do not care," urged Ann. "Let us just get out of here before they catch us."

"West, then," said Kate. "Let us go."

"Follow me," said Jake, exiting the room.

A few stretches of hallway and they stood before a locked door. Jake fished out a key and led them into a warehouse dominated by rows of ancient automobiles and trucks that had been converted into light armored vehicles and transports.

"The terrain will be rough and we will not have any engineers with us, so let us take that one over there," said Jake. The vehicle he referred to had once been a four-wheel drive, large-capacity passenger vehicle. Now the windows had been replaced with armor, the top sported a machine gun, and a mortar had been mounted in the back. Food, water, and ammunition was stashed inside, but there was still plenty of room for three people.

Inside Jake showed the women how to strap on their safety harnesses. Then he set the vehicle in motion, in a few quick moves placing it in front of a small trailer. "There is alcohol in that trailer. I will hook it up and be right back."

Soon Jake opened the warehouse door and they emerged from the City of Zion.

"I am going to take the same roads our army planned to take, at least for now. They will take us out of Zion pretty quickly, maybe before the sun comes up. I want you to watch me, though. Watch how I operate this vehicle. As soon as the sun comes up I will want one of you to drive it. That way I will be able to watch from the top and use our weapons if anyone tries to stop us. There is not much in Zion that is a match for this vehicle except the other ones like it. Well, there are the tanks, but they are too slow to get near us."

Chapter 24

The Child who had been standing guard duty and allowed Kate and Ann into the military area had nothing else to think about until her shift ended at 2 A.M. Her name was Marie Juanita Gomez and she had been in the Cleveland Police force in her past incarnation, hence her selection for military service under Mary Mother of God. With her replacement she decided to report the matter to Mother Angela. Since there was no telephone available near the post, only a button that would signal a general alarm and wake everyone up, Marie walked to Mother Angela's sleeping quarters.

"Mother, Mother, please wake up," pleaded Marie until Mother Angela was awake.

"What is it child," muttered the mother, finally.

"During my guard shift two Children, Mary Kate Ashton and Ann Swanson came with orders from Mother Tanya Jeane telling them to report to Jake Thompson. I know I had orders to not let anyone by, but they had orders."

"That is all right honey, I am sure it is all right, Mother Tanya Jeane probably just forgot to inform me. Still, I had better call her right now. If we are going to be an army we have to keep our signals straight."

The bell rang a long time before Mother Tanya Jeane answered the phone harshly.

"Mary Kate Ashton and Ann Swanson? I surely did not issue such orders. You had better go and find them right away. Search your area and I will check for them in the Temple."

Within a half hour they realized that Jake and the Children were gone along with one of the fighting vehicles. "Ann Swanson was causing trouble not that long ago. Jake knew her from when he worked in the Temple of the Resurrection. It is the work of the devil, that is for sure. Mary Kate is highly trained, we need her back, and replacing that armored car would not be easy. I think we should wake everyone up and start our mission to Mexico. It is very possible we will catch up with the apostates along the way."

"Look, couldn't we call Gideon and have them try to stop them? They have to pass right by Gideon."

"You can try, but I don't think our soldiers in Gideon are a match for the machine gun mounted on that jeep. They'll be on their guard, too, and can just go off the road."

"Surely they are not going to take our route to Mexico. Surely they will head out into the wilderness?"

"We can follow the vehicle's tracks. If they go off our path we will have to decide at that point how to pursue them. But they are not stupid. They cannot survive by themselves. They will take their chances with the Mexicans. Wake everyone up; I want to leave in half an hour. I will wake up the Council; I am sure they will approve my decision. Well, do not just stand there, get moving!"

The Army of Mary the Mother of God left Resurrection City at 5:25 A.M.

Chapter 25

Mary Kate sat in the front with Jake; Ann sat behind.

"First look back to see if anyone is following us. Roll down your windows ... see that thing there? Turn it counter-clockwise."

Ann got it right the first time; Kate tried turning the end of the handle like it was a dial before imitating Ann. It was hard to tell anything with the wind rushing by and the bouncing of the jeep.

"What are we looking for?" said Ann.

"Lights that look like they are following us," bellowed Jake, trying to view back through his rear-view mirrors.

"I do not see anyone."

"Okay, we'll check again later."

"What is 'we'll?'" asked Kate.

"It is what is called a contraction, a word from two words. It stands for 'we will.' The Mothers banned contractions. I will explain later, this isn't the time for grammar lessons. What I'm holding with my hands is called the steering wheel. If I turn it to the right, like this, the car goes to the right, and to the left, like this it goes to the left. Mostly the idea is to go straight on the road, but sometimes you have to make turns. Now look down where my feet are. There are three pedals..."

For a while the women watched Jake. Then he brought the car to a halt and got out. "Come on, get out," he said. The lights of Resurrection City had already faded in the distance. There was no sign of pursuit. They got back in the car.

"So let's assume we'll get out of Zion alive. The way I see it we have two basic choices. We try to find a place where we can live in isolation. If we do that then you are right, our best bet is to go east, where water is not a problem. We could head south too, because then winter isn't as big of a problcm. On the other hand there's a good chance we'll simply starve to death. We don't know if we can find food growing wild, and we don't know if we can grow anything. You say you brought seeds?"

"Corn, barley, wheat, three kinds of beans," answered Kate.

"Well, we can try. The other option is to go join the Mexicans. That would be a long and dangerous trip. But obviously the Mexicans are growing food, so if they are friendly we would be better off."

"I am afraid they will be like the Mothers," said Ann. "They will want to tell us what to do and think. I suppose they are not exactly like the Mothers, but they could be different and still order us around."

"I say let us take our chances without the Mexicans," said Kate.

"There is one other consideration," Jake stated. "Zion is sending an army to Mexico to conquer the Mexicans. Zion is also planning on establishing a colony halfway between the two states. If the Mothers control Mexico, they will probably be able to just keep expanding. It might be a long time before they found us, but they would find us eventually. There's a moral argument too. We know that the Mexicans are going to be attacked by Zion. We cannot assume they are bad people. Even if we do not want to live with them, we should warn them."

"What if they force us to join them when we go to warn them?" asked Ann.

"We should be able to circumvent that. We have some powerful weaponry on this vehicle. We should be able to find a lone Mexican and talk to her or him, get an idea of what is going on there. We can sneak up on them and observe them. If they have a bunch of people bossing everyone else around then we can just leave them to their fate."

"Jake is right, Ann," said Kate. "We have to at least try. Anyway, I have been confined to tiny rooms all my life. Let us see what we can see, even if it has become a great big wasteland. Maybe we will find I place we would like to live."

"Alright, I guess. We are not even out of Zion yet, are we?"

"No. And see this needle, how it is getting near the E? E stands for empty, which means we will have to stop and take gas out of that trailer in the back and put it in the tank. In fact let us do that now, it is getting light and I would rather do it while we are hard to spot. I'm going to pull off the road. Notice how I shift down through the gears, pushing the clutch in for each change, with my foot off the gas pedal. We will go behind that abandoned building over there. Now that I am going good and slow it will be easy to turn."

They came to a halt behind the building. From the remains Jake knew it had been a little strip mall, probably just a gas station and grocery store. The set up for the gas trailer was not convenient: they had to fill up their gas bottle two gallons at a time and then pour it into the tank of the jeep.

"What about food," said Kate.

"I would like to concentrate on getting out of Zion," said Jake.

"We could at least chew on some of the wheat berries," suggested Ann, who was quite hungry.

"Fine. Now, Kate, you can take a turn driving. I want to be able to use the machine gun if we run into trouble. This road goes right by Gideon, so we will get off it and try to go around. I will show you on the map. Now, this is a machine gun. These things here are bullets. They have gunpowder in them and when it explodes this metal part here shoots out really fast and if it hits a person it will kill them. It is the kind of thing everyone was using during the Apocalypse. This barrel is where the bullets come out..."

There was considerable light, although the sun had not yet breached the horizon, when they started off again. Jake sat by Kate, who had considerable difficulty coordinating her driving. But once she was on the road and just had to drive straight she got the hang of shifting gears pretty quickly. Jake's main worry was that he would miss the turn off before Gideon.

Ann was ostensibly helping as a lookout. It was great fun, riding along the highway in a bumpy jeep. No one seemed to be pursuing them. The landscape was desolate, with only the remains of pre-apocalypse civilization to attract her attention.

Jake tried to use the map to keep track of where they were, but there were no road signs, so he was just guessing. Well before they got to Gideon he got down beside Kate, had her slow to a crawl, and turned off onto a side road. This road was in terrible repair so they went along much slower, seldom getting up to twenty miles per hour.

A half hour later, they saw the road block.

"We could try to fight them, but this is a four wheel drive vehicle designed to go off the road, and those cars of theirs are probably hardly fit to drive on the road. We'll be in real trouble if they get off a lucky shot and take out a tire or that tank of alcohol we are hauling. Do you think you can drive okay? Maybe I should drive and forget about the gun."

"I will be fine."

"Wait, I'm going to get out a rifle for Ann. No, see that dirt path there? Go down that. I have an idea."

Jake tried to explain the rifle to Ann while they jolted along the path, which quickly tapered out into the hardened landscape.

"Now head around that hill," Jake instructed. The hill was just a rise, not much higher than needed to protect them from view.

Sure enough, the two cars that had been blocking the road were making their way across the fields, trying to head them off. A number of people on foot remained back at the roadblock.

"Head straight towards them, parallel to the road. Go slow, first gear, maybe ten miles per hour. When I tell you make a sharp right turn back towards the road and accelerate. Go right past the road until I tell you."

The Mothers' cars came towards them and someone leaned out a window and fired a shot. Jake was amazed at their stupidity; he could easily have killed them all with the machine gun. Instead he waited until they were about fifty yards away and screamed "Turn, turn, turn."

Kate turned the wheel to the right, went past her mark, swerved a bit and finally got herself headed in the right direction. In the meantime she had slowed to a crawl and Jake was yelling "faster, faster, faster."

Kate kicked the gas pedal and methodically went up through the gears. The jeep bumped wildly over the uneven ground.

Ann was pleased with the maneuver, which left the Mothers' cars well behind them, though not very far behind. As they approached the road Jake fired the machine gun over the heads of the people at the roadblock. They dove for cover. Then Jake came down beside Kate. "Whoa! That is fast enough. Try to curve gradually left now, making a big arc until we get back to the road."

Back up top victory seemed near. One of the pursuers was far behind and seemed to have stopped. The other was well back and losing ground quickly. In seconds they were past the roadblock, and soon after that back on the road.

"Hopefully that's the end of it," said Jake.

"I did not get to fire the rifle," said Ann.

"Okay, aim it back along the road. Safety off. Remember it will kick back. Now squeeze the trigger."

The rifle roared, nearly knocking Ann over. Jake laughed out loud. He had not laughed out loud since the Apocalypse.

"I guess soon it will be your turn to drive," he said.

"It should not be hard. I must have driven before the Apocalypse. They just forgot to have Remembrance lessons about it."

Anarchist Fiction From III Publishing

The Last Days of Christ the Vampire by J.G. Eccarius
ISBN 0-9622937-0-9 192 pages, 4¼ x 7" $7.00

The book that broke the silence about the vampiric nature of Jesus Christ and his fundamentalist zombies. Jesus has set his sights on converting some teenagers in Providence, Rhode Island, but instead they resist and set out to hunt him down before he can release his Apocalypse upon the world. Arguably the best religious satire of the 20th century. Jesus Lives; vampires never die.

Virgintooth by Mark Ivanhoe
ISBN: 0-9622937-3-3 192 pages, 4¼ x 7" $7.00

There is no escape: at death every soul is swallowed up into the abysmal hunger of the feral vampires. Elizabeth, however, has not exactly died: she has been made into a vampire. Now she has not only the problems she had when alive, and of avoiding the feral vampires, but she must also get along with the other human vampires. At times terrifying, at times hysterically funny, Virgintooth will enlighten and delight you.

My Journey With Aristotle to the Anarchist Utopia
by Graham Purchase
ISBN: 0-9622937-6-8 128 pages, 4¼ x 7" $7.00

When Tom emerges from a thousand-year-sleep in a mine he encounters Aristotle, who leads him down to Bear City. There he sees how human life can be organized without government or bosses of any kind. The inhabitants of Bear City live in harmony with nature and one another, yet have a highly developed civilization. It's a journey worth taking, and at the same time a send up of Plato's The Republic.

(continued next page)

Geminga, Sword of the Shining Path by Melvin Litton
ISBN 0-9622937-4-1 5½ x 8½", 256 pages
$9.95

In a world poised between a superstitious past and a surreal future of bioengineering, virtual reality and artificial consciousness, Geminga surfs on the winds of the present. A product of genetic engineering, this bird has been trained since infancy to assassinate the enemies of Peru's Sendero Luminoso. Now she's come with her best friend, Jimmy the Snake, to California Norte.

This'll Kill Ya by Harry Willson
ISBN 0-9622937-2-5 192 pages 4¼ x 7"
$6.00

The anti-censorship thriller that will have you laughing out loud and examining your own reactions to materials that surely should be censored. Caution: If you believe that words can be used as weapons to harm people, reading these pages may be hazardous to your health. Willson has a devilishly delightful sense of humor that should place him in everyone's library.

We Should Have Killed the King by J.G. Eccarius
ISBN 0-9622937-1-7 192 pages 4¼ x 7"
$5.00

Jack Straw and hundreds of thousands of other English peasants rebelled against their overlords in 1381, killing nobles, lawyers and tax collectors. Ultimately they were crushed, but the spirit of rebellion was reborn in America in the punk/anarchist movement during the 1980's and Jack Straw was there. A stunning look about the underground in the USA.

non-fiction:

Vampires or Gods by William Meyers

ISBN 0-9622937-5-X 192 pages, 8.5 x 11"
$15.00

Vampires living thousands of years, commanding legions of human worshippers. The stuff of horror novels? No these vampires are right out of ancient history books. Every major ancient civilization was associated with an immortal claiming to be a god. Egypt had Osiris, who rose from the dead after his body was hacked to pieces and buried in separate places. He reigned for 3000 years. Asia Minor had Cybele, whose followers fed her their blood. She was thousands of years old when she saved Rome from Hannibal's army in 204 B.C. Greece had Dionysus and Hercules, Rome had Quirinus, and the list goes on. Altogether the most powerful conspiracy in the history of the world. With illustrations and extensive quotations from the ancient historians.

Look for these titles at bookstores; they can always order you a copy if you can't find them in stock. Actually, a lot of corporations don't like our message so...

To order direct from III Publishing send cash, or check or money order for the listed price (postage & handling is free! in the US; add $2 elsewhere) made out to III Publishing, P.O. Box 1581 Gualala, CA 95445. Or send $1.00 for an up-to-date catalog.

THE STAKE

Humor and horror for a dying planet

Our magazine will give you a dose of weirdness on a semi-regular basis.

"Bill Meyers proves that there is something more scarring and lasting than bad drug trips, Viet Nam flashbacks and Maude re-runs. That would, of course, be a Catholic School upringing. Bill publishes a 64-page short story bonanza, **The Stake**, devoting a suspiciously substantial amount of ink to stories laden with crucifixes, rosaries, killer nuns and horny priests. Most of the stories have a Twilight Zone-esque spin, like the role-reversal yarn about the successful businessman who devises a bloody solution to the homeless problem, only to find himself rummaging through the dumpsters, a victim of his own handiwork. The Stake also boasts regular features, including book reviews, the ongoing wacky adventures of the Snopeses, a letters section and (a favorite among serial killers) the infamous "Severed Heads" column. - Joe Bob Briggs

"The Stake is an appealingly produced, wide-ranging, and often very effective satire magazine. Subtitled 'Humor & Horror for a Dying Planet,' it seems eager to take on authority and official versions of reality whenever possible and frequently ventures into the realm of the fantastic without breaking stride. Religion, government, high finance, complaints about welfare and the dehumanization technical advances can promote are but a few of the subjects skewered.

My personal favorite was the lead piece, a single page gem on priestly Celibacy from 'Our Vatican Correspondent.' It's an almost flawless, devastatingly on-the-mark shot at religious power structure busily rewriting history and doubletalking its way around threats to its legitimacy...Highly recommended."

— Scavenger's Newsletter